ROSE ALLEY

ROSE ALLEY

Jeremy M. Davies

COUNTERPATH PRESS

DENVER

2009

Counterpath Press
Denver, Colorado
www.counterpathpress.org

Printed in Canada

Library of Congress Cataloging-in-Publication Data

Davies, Jeremy M., 1978–
    Rose Alley / Jeremy M. Davies.
        p.   cm.
    ISBN 978-1-933996-13-4 (pbk. : alk. paper)
    1. Cinematography—France—Fiction.   2. Motion pictures—
Production and direction—France—Fiction.   3. Motion picture
actors and actresses—Fiction.   4. Motion picture producers and
directors—Fiction.   5. Protest movements—France—1960–1970—
Fiction.   6. Paris (France)—Fiction.   I. Title.
PS3604.A9537R67 2009
813'.6—dc22

                                                          2008053277

Distributed by Small Press Distribution (www.spdbooks.org)

For SEF.

As ever.

As always.

More or less.

CONTENTS

The authentic experiences of the nineteen sixties will all be composed of memories that will be a little bit mistaken.

— F. T. CASTLE

We'll get there in the end, with a little method.

— R. PINGET

1
Evelyn Nevers

They shot her screen test in Paris, where I've never been, in the private room of the café Tout Va Bien, in the Latin Quarter, newly paved in tar, and still lewd that winter with debris from the blockades of stacked cobblestones—centuries old, pried right off the streets—and the stink of some secret catastrophe. It was January and she was twenty-two and had done three pictures to date (Italian sex farces: too explicit for first-run houses, too tepid for connoisseurs), all produced by Prosper Sforza. He'd earmarked her for his new project because he was sleeping with her. He wanted to be kept on. He was thirty-three years her elder and hadn't figured out that she loved him. She didn't know it herself.

A saltcellar painted in red varnish and creamy with English grease, inherited by her family from a vicar in Leeds—who as an airman slept out the Occupation wrapped in parachute in their barn, nightly engaging in nervous frottage through the silk of it with her mother come to check that his legs were mending—had attained a retrospective significance as Prosper's analogue, and

haunted her dreams and meals. Every new and humiliating role
he devised for her, every vacant insinuation that came out of his
mouth, hit her, lately, in two places at once: in her head, an ortho-
dox oval, and in her belly, a modest bowl.

Sforza's stomach was flat and hairless but soft to touch, with
the feel of fatness. His was an adolescent's slenderness, retained
to middle age, threatening to swell if not well tended. He ate a
lot, but not often, and then only meat: proud of his figure, eager
to show it, and already three-quarters beef and mutton—or so
Evelyn calculated privately.

She had cause to complain of him almost daily in her diary
1969–1970, a perfect-bound college notebook, six by ten, on loan
to me from her youngest son Joss (short for Jocelyn, gay as three
grapes and practicing law in Toronto; he won't get it back).

Evelyn kept very strict accounts, having a weakness for lists
and preferring them to declarative statements, totaling her daily
expenditures each morning in the left-hand margin while listing
in the right the setting and the prominent characters present in
her last night's dreams (carnival, seaside, the wastes of Jupiter,
Prosper, an attic room). Among more substantive minutiae—such
as her hatred of Paris in the wintertime, her desire to study medicine, and her muddled transcription of a poem by an American
author entitled "Woman Irritable Because of Her Menses" that
wouldn't see legitimate publication for almost a decade—the first
twelve pages of the journal also record the date and time of her
test (left margin), as well as the roster of persons present (right),
substantiating the particulars taken from Sforza's often baffling business records, filled as they are with detailed pen-and-
ink sketches of what he referred to as *uccelli* (winged phalluses of
Classical origin, precise to the last vein and feather) and outright

paranoid fantasy. That he had fucked her to a froth at their hotel on the Place Vendôme minutes before their arriving at the café— in separate cars, he in great cheer, still brushing his teeth—goes unrecorded.

Also present at the Tout Va Bien, if in significantly lower spirits, were the American screenwriter Myrna Krause, English director Selwyn Wexler, editor Eugenia Sleck, designer Ephraim Bueno, stars Archibald and Millicent Harkness—the latter still bandaged from her contretemps during the worst of the riots— and lighting-cameraman Raoul Foche, with his spring-driven 8mm Bolex, lamps, bulbs, box of lenses, and Russian Blue kitten Yevgennie. These are the names I can be sure of.

The writer and director weren't speaking. Wexler and Krause each read their own issues of *Cahiers du Cinéma*: last year's and last month's, respectively. It took Prosper's entrance, his burying both hands in Myrna's short dirty hair, to make the assembly animate.

Myrna let him scratch her scalp. Nothing short of violence would have stopped him. Myrna was tiny and untidy—she didn't shave or wash. Her college French was like Japanese, all adverbs and no pronouns. How could Sforza stand to touch her, even in jest? Evelyn supposed in her diary that he must need to feel every woman he met was *accessible*. Prosper got his toothbrush out of his mouth where he'd been chewing on it and stood it up like a pen in a pocket of his blazer before shaking everybody's hands.

Evelyn knew Wexler didn't want her in his movie. He hadn't even wanted to shoot it in Paris, but Sforza claimed to be a tax exile: he'd be arrested at customs if he crossed the Channel. The Latin Quarter's cobblestones, narrow streets, and lax film-permit policy had all been cited in the negotiations as good reasons for Wexler's making the compromise; and anyhow, John Wilmot, the

Earl of Rochester—the smutty Restoration poet and the putative subject of their film—had been exiled to France once too, when a variety of offenses to King Charles made his presence at court intolerable. A year later and shooting still hadn't started, and there was asphalt instead of cobblestones and graffiti everywhere (*The walls have ears—your ears have walls*) and gendarmes on twenty-four-hour patrol. Rather than Fonda or Bardot or Harkness (and here was Millicent, like her husband a little old for the role, but present and willing and already under contract) to play Lady Elizabeth Wilmot, Rochester's long-suffering wife, Wexler was being thrown this baggage from the nudie flicks, looking like she'd stood too close to a kiln, stared too long at an eclipse, or been shaved every inch beneath her eyebrows with rubbing alcohol and a match—or so Evelyn lamented to her diary. Wexler spoke less every time she met him. Everyone could see he was expecting a disaster: he telegraphed it like a maiden aunt, sighing, sniffing, rolling his eyes. The morning of the screen test he didn't say a word. She'd never before taken her clothing off in front of anyone so inconclusive. She wanted him to like her. She came out of her cab in a surplice and sandals.

I've reviewed the 8mm footage shot by Foche more than twenty times, and have yet to discern any thematic relevance to Krause and Wexler's script, set in 1679 London. The film resembles nothing so much as a particularly clumsy five-minute stroke-loop, still common at the time, and is differentiated from these only by its date-stamp, burned by the laboratory on every frame at Prosper Sforza's insistence. There are numerous abrupt and puzzling close-ups of Evelyn's face, eyes, shoulders, and feet. She is hairless and not very muscular. At thirty-eight seconds she seems to be dismissing suggestions from off-camera. She laughs at one-minute-thirty, and at three-minutes-five Yevgennie scoots into frame at the lower right. Evelyn bends over to pick him up and the camera shakes (and then stays crooked for the duration) as Raoul offers anxiously to relieve her of his cat. Evelyn refuses and cradles Yevgennie like a newborn. Running the film frame by frame here reveals that the feline rogue does indeed lick at her left nipple, inadvertently perverse, though she pretends not to notice and laughs again (at four minutes exactly), this time at Raoul's increasing anxiety on the kitten's behalf. At four-min-utes-fifteen the animal performs an act of kitty-magic and turns over and around before Evelyn knows he's stirred. Yevgennie then flutters onto her shoulder, and as she reacts to his escape, behemoth-slow, he sinks every infant claw into her skin, draw-ing dollops of blood like charcoal syrup on my improvised screen (bed sheet, thumbtacks).

Whatever her fans might say, her posture and expression of as-tonishment here are the most erotic items in the test. The film runs only ten seconds more, with Yevgennie hanging off Evelyn's hide in terror, sensing her determination to dash his brains out on the floor. Raoul dropped his camera, smashing the lens, vaulting over to take his cat from Evelyn before the fatal blow could be dealt. She cried nude in the women's toilet while "C'est d'la faute à tes yeux" played, all treble, over the café speakers.

She knew how to hate. At the age of ten she'd developed the habit of eating raw salt from the vicar's red cellar; she'd lick her right index finger and dip it in salt and happily lick it off again; she did it on every trip through the kitchen, while her mother rolled the dough or reheated the coffee or cooked what she called spa-ghetti but was really rice-noodles—from a dry goods store where she could buy Moroccan cigarettes—swirled in a compote of fresh

garlic and what Monsieur Nevers called guinea red (an expediency of translation), served with peeled tomatoes and cheese and
buttered rolls. The business with the salt frightened her parents
for no reason they could articulate, and they soon forbade her to
have salt at all, except on beef and soup. Evelyn was their first and
only child; they didn't understand that their prohibition made the
saltcellar irresistible.

Evelyn took to eating whole spoonfuls of salt when their backs
were turned. She didn't even like the taste anymore. She stopped
defecating and drank twenty-four glasses of water at every meal.
Her parents removed salt from their diets completely and hid the
saltcellar from Leeds in their modest wine cellar, though Evelyn
found it and spent her leisure time underground dissolving slugs
and licking her finger and urinating on her father's delectable
bundle of newspapers dating from the Liberation.

So Madame Nevers destroyed their salt: every grain in the
house into the sink and cold water turned on top of it. It melted
like sand. Her husband began dining alone in town and threatened to smash the empty saltcellar: a gift he'd never been comfortable with, and that now seemed positively demonic. Evelyn
knew how to hate, and thus began letting boys watch her piss on
the Liberation for pennies, which she would then use to buy her
own two-pound bags of salt; filling the vicar herself and dipping
her finger like she used to, parents none the wiser, happily misled.
She was found out only when she collapsed from cramps on her
twelfth birthday and was rushed to the town doctor. She had the
pulse-rate of a sparrow, was developing two or three stomach ul-
cers, and the doctor didn't care to guess whether her kidneys were
on the point of dissolving.

But Evelyn didn't know that Monsieur Nevers also knew how to hate. He proved it by locking her in the wine cellar with the vicar full to brimming of salt from the market and with the information that this was her birthday dinner, and that he would probably murder her with fat packing twine if he found so much as a granule left over come morning. He also knew how to hate, but the gene had truly flowered in Evelyn. She took off her twelve-year-old's clothing and squatted by the vicar to rub the salt into her stomach and sides, into her armpits and the crevices between her toes. When she was done with her skin and hair she set to work on the mucous membranes: up her nose, in her eyes, deep in her ears. She put some up her ass and rubbed it vigorously on and in her cunt, which never really did look the same. There were piles of the stuff left over come morning: on the floor, on her body, and even in the vicar, but Monsieur Nevers didn't murder his daughter—he drove her to his hospital and watched them boil the salt out of her, then sat with her in the burn ward until she could sleep. Not to be maudlin, but when one of his tears got into his mouth, he had to run to the washroom and vomit. Nine years later Evelyn played Lot's wife (as well as one of his salacious daughters) in Sforza's nudie biblical epic *Gli Occhi del Dio* (*Two by Two*), an anthology of burlesques of the seven most sordid Old Testament episodes he could call to mind without having recourse to a Bible.

The second picture she made with Sforza was called *Un Mondo Senza Amore* (*Let Me Shut off Delight*), concerning millionaire archfiend Bodkin Diabolik's scheme to doom the human race to extinction via a machine capable of extinguishing the sexual appetite of every mammal on the planet with disorienting electromagnetic pulses. It was during this shoot that Sforza and Evelyn first went to bed, and around this time that Myrna Krause collaborated with Selwyn Wexler on their first and only film to date,

the twenty-minute short *Muzeum*. This was a collection of miniatures, thirteen still lifes in thirteen continuous shots, ninety seconds in duration each. An elaborate system of eleven predeter-
mined categories, subcategories, and corresponding lists of objects
matching each classification—either likely, unlikely, invented, or
inconceivable—was coauthored by Krause and Wexler and used to
determine which subjects were to be filmed.

Two dice were rolled, rolled again, and rolled again. Myrna
and Selwyn sought out each object their system named and didn't
grumble when they were ordered to find providence, an active
beehive, tetanus, or a tin roof. They shot what they could and improvised the rest. "Perplexity," for instance, was a shot of Myrna's
scalp, so pale as to be bloodless, and so close to the camera it came
across like a family of gnats on paper. Selwyn filmed each subject with a camera borrowed from the BFI, soldered the stock together, and screened the results for Myrna, who then sat in his
bath until she had forced herself to write up some connective tis-
sue, a narrative that would indict every item in turn and force the
mute fragments to tell a story. She wanted Wexler to come in on
her while she was still undressed; Wexler waiting watching television thought of nothing else; and it took two hours altogether for
the script to be written. They fell asleep at his mother's kitchen
table as Myrna, robed, read it aloud from her sopping notebook.

Myrna had a beautiful speaking voice and so was enlisted to
narrate her story over some scratchy Bolshevik-era Bartók snip-
pets and so be the film's soundtrack as well as its author. The final
product played well at a festival and even got aired on BBC2, but
was publicized in both instances as *Museum With a Zee*—due to
several obvious miscommunications—and Wexler nearly killed

Myrna and himself driving home drunk from an awards ceremony at which he had been gently teased for his pretensions.

This at any rate was what Evelyn knew about the two Anglophones, dabbing her wounds with paper in the women's toilet, not allowing them to scab and stop bleeding. Wexler had sent Myrna in after her because she had a beautiful speaking voice and was the only woman present besides the waitress out front, who was too busy with the morning rush to be bothered, and anyway had upset him several months earlier by pinching his backside, possibly at Sforza's instigation, possibly for money. Myrna's voice had sounded strange to her own ears coming over ripped speakers in an art-house cinema when her and Wexler's short had screened, and also strange to her echoed in any tiled bathroom—the Tout Va Bien toilet no exception—but she could understand that people found it to be a pleasantly resonant sound and hoped that if she were to hear it coming out of another woman, she herself would find it attractive. Evelyn's voice was average in tone and unappealing musically. She took a delight in sibilants and fricatives quite abnormal for a provincial Frenchwoman, possibly due to the time she'd spent in Italy, possibly due to a desire to spit on every person she saw.

Another thing that was strange to Myrna was seeing Evelyn's body at such close quarters. Her interest in pornography and lurid media of any stripe amounted to a hobby. She alone among her colleagues in the café had sat through all two hundred and seventy minutes of Evelyn's three completed films, and she alone among her colleagues in the café had experienced something akin to arousal during the shooting of the screen test, though this was more to do with the science of iconography than an authentic desire to put her hands on the body thus displayed.

Evelyn sent Myrna back to get her handbag, which had been left in the private room on the long table with folding legs that Sforza, Myrna, Wexler, and Foche had rested their elbows on while she'd undressed. Inside were Mercurochrome and bandages, as well as Italian condoms, British cookies, French pencils, colonial cigarettes, and her 1969–1970 diary (bound in Holyoke, Massachusetts). Myrna watched with interest the peregrinations of the flesh of the thighs of Lot's wife, the elbows of Super-Agent Soixante-Neuf, the tits of Helen of Troy, as Evelyn washed and disinfected her punctured shoulder and much of the rest of her torso as well. She wanted to make everyone wait.

She was wondering what bacteria might have been on Yevgennie's claws that had now been injected into her bloodstream. Foche was certain to be filthy: all his type were. They lived in their own refuse, didn't shave or wash; even a cat couldn't keep clean in the reek of it. Evelyn was sure she felt feverish. Monsieur Nevers had been a hospital orderly and had fostered Evelyn's longstanding interest in medicine by his teasing threats to infect her with any one of the renowned diseases he could partake of daily in the course of his rounds. Her studying was desultory, but she blamed her parents' breakup for her failure to enter medical school. She was training as a nurse in Paris and sharing a room with three other women when a short man on a moped spotted her crossing a street against the light and asked if she would like to make some extra money modeling. She wasn't interested in dissuading him and rode off with her arms around his waist.

The man was Mercury to Sforza's Jupiter. It was 1966 and the mogul was still allowed in England. He tried to seduce her immediately and she demurred by deliberately misconstruing his actions as a Mediterranean attempt to make her more comfortable in the passenger seat of his Jaguar. In London, where Myrna and Wexler were just meeting, she and he played nightlong and nightly games of attack and retreat alone over cocktails after photo shoots for his men's magazine *The Connoisseur*. Evelyn was a nice girl and Sforza so tormented that she did him Roman favors on several occasions, years before any actual coition occurred, and they became great friends during this intermission, though Sforza showed no favoritism on the set.

Evelyn had a trick for getting through the photo shoots, and eventually her film scenes as well. Not that they were excruciating. She wasn't too ashamed. The real problem was boredom, the repertoire of acceptable expressions and motions in the context of a Sforza job being fairly limited. The system she devised was this: she would find out from the photographer or director what kinds of shot were likely to be taken during the next day's work—close-ups of her face? her chest? her face and someone else's chest?— and study up in her anatomy text about the organs and processes hidden in those areas by the skin the audience paid to see. Most importantly, she studied the pathologies of these body segments: what could and did go wrong. If she touched her cheek (or it was touched by a colleague) she would picture the veins and muscles fulminating underneath. If this nerve were serrated by a knife or nail you'd never smile or squint again. Every eyeblink could be made a sizzling ordeal, or else like long neglected roll-up blinds your lids could be made to hang limp and loose, forever closed and wetly rumpled. A lens pointed at her feet brought to mind rare bony protrusions that made walking impossible—every surface able to draw blood, even carpets, even cotton—the leg and arm muscles warping over time to support the odd stances the sufferer assumes to minimize his discomfort, limbs eventually looking like they belong on some other animal, something that climbs or crawls or flies. Scenes of simulated sex made her think of vulval insect bites in tropical climes, the various cancers and polyps like tusks or withered and innovative new appendages seen to have emanated from the skin around the scrotum or labia, as though the body were seeking an alternate means to acquit itself of a burdensome responsibility.

She still used this trick of hers, and it gave her face a paradoxically winsome air while she worked. She'd done it during the screen test, touching her sides and stomach with her fingertips while Sforza encouraged her to turn around or pull up her hair and Foche followed along, whirring. No one could have guessed.

She thought: here is my small intestine. If it were punctured by a bullet or knife, shit would leak into my bloodstream and choke me to death. My body is a carrier and producer of poisons. Eventually the processes that keep the poisons separate will break down, and the contents of my body will mix. It is only by their differentiation that I stay alive and individual. Old age will mix me and then I'll have taken a step toward becoming muck like the humus I walk on in the garden or that black Raoul Foche lives and sleeps in with his wife and kid and cat in their perfumed shithole in Montparnasse. Scratches are the world and its dirt mixing with my system. Prosper fucks me, and the vibrations themselves are entropic and hasten my demise. Selwyn Wexler in his hotel room gets a hard-on thinking about me and the blood that goes into his cock could probably be put to better use. I touch my belly and I am touching a time bomb whose detonation will leave me without recourse.

2
Prosper Sforza

His full name was Sidney Edmond Jocelyn Prosper Sforza, and he was born in February, in Paris, at the start of the First World War. His grandfather raised him while his papa was in the trenches and mother beside herself worrying. The old man was of uncertain origins; he would only say that he had no royal blood and had come down from a restless northern land, which little Sforza took to mean that the country itself was mobile, like a lily pad, leaving him determined to track it down and hop aboard when he grew up. He developed a fondness for maps, though they were not to be trusted, showing states stiff and static as jigsaw pieces rather than arcs and orbits and educated guesses. He started a collection and just as soon forgot it; later a few were framed and hung at the Tout Va Bien.

Zeydie Sforza had been in show business; Prosper could say it was in his blood. The old man had made a fortune traveling the cities of Europe, enjoying his greatest successes playing the grotesque stage Jews who were at that time as familiar to theatergoers as Harlequin or Pierrot. He'd spoken through enormous wax noses, wore molting purple ermine, and carried bags of clamorous iron coins. His audiences were terrorized, hiccoughing with laughter, and he became exceedingly popular. Demand was so great that he hired a real Jew to sort the invitations he was receiving. Soon Sforza was so acclaimed that he was suspected of cheating: of being an honest-to-God Hebe himself, putting one over on the goyim. He retired immediately and settled in London, where he met Prosper's grandmother, an Italian immigrant selling scarves on the street. She married him despite his age and race and thus began the family tradition of assuming that he *had* been Jewish all along—the wag. By the logic of the period, this made her and her children equally suspect—even to themselves—and they accepted this stigma with the incurious good humor that, along with a certain tendency towards prognathism, was their real paternal inheritance.

Zeydie gambled away much of his fortune and fled to the continent to escape a constellation of debts and bad checks—an act his grandson would be doomed to repeat. He and his wife arrived in time for the end of the Franco-Prussian War and lived through the Commune of 1871, a disaster Flaubert blamed on universal suffrage, commenting, "What a throw-back! What savages!" Sforza was an enthusiastic communard and ate dog without complaint during the siege of Paris. He got his wife with child for the new society and wept when Versailles took the city back and bloodied it with reprisals.

With what little money remained he bought the three-story building on the Left Bank that would house the Tout Va Bien in fifty years' time, to help his son make a start in the trade of his choice. Sforza the Younger set himself up as a designer and caster of movable type, specializing in Greek and Hebrew characters, while the paterfamilias walked from Paris to Modena to bury his wife. He returned by train, went up to the top floor, and absented himself from worldly affairs in a rococo wing chair with velvet upholstery and the heads of sea lions carved on the armrests. He remained for years in a paralytic melancholy from which he only recovered when he was given a credulous grandson.

By this time the type business had folded. Scholars and their publishers found themselves peculiarly unable to trust a Jew to make letters for their Bibles and *Odyssey*s. The storefront and workshop were rented out to a small-time printer and publisher of inferior limited-run translations of erotic ghost stories from the English and Spanish. Sforza the Younger got himself hired there, in that husk of his old business, setting type he found garish and casting clean sturdy stereotype plates from his work to facilitate rapid turnover. Proper proofing and spacing pleasant to the eye were all secondary concerns to the proprietor, who spent the bulk of his production budget seeking out new manuscripts and trans- lators—putting a premium on texts written by "liberated women" who preferred to remain anonymous, and literate world travelers who could tell him where and what a perineum was without hesi- tation. He was a connoisseur.

Prosper's father began to pursue the proprietor's daughter, who made sporadic visits to the shop with her mother, a sweet-natured woman who'd been led to believe that her husband made his liv- ing reviving classics of Symbolist poetry. The daughter was taller than Sforza by a head, wore her hair in the oriental style, and had broken off her last engagement on account of the fiancé's smirk- ing at her solemn request to give a man she mistook for the ailing Oscar Wilde every cent he might have on his person.

Sforza's intentions were not wholly honorable; Mlle Connoisseur was lovely as a lamppost, but it was her family's press he was after. She might have realized this sooner if an inexplicable preoccupation with Sforza's rumored Jewishness had not overwhelmed her celebrated perspicacity. She began to dream at night of being Queen Esther, or Judith with her sword, and heard secret voices telling her that her real homeland was the desert. So strong was the compulsion to become something unfamiliar, she persuaded herself she had always been a Jew at heart; that Sforza had been provided so she might again find the path to a righteous life. She had never seen a circumcised penis—had in fact only seen her father's (and perhaps one other), and medical circumcision hadn't yet been accepted by your poorer sort of bourgeois—so now burned to see one, making it out to be a novelty, and telling Sforza just that, being a liberated lady of her father's design. Sforza stole money from the elder Sforza to get the operation and as a result drove Mlle Connoisseur mad with desire by turning indifferent to her advances on account of the pain. It lasted months, and by the time he'd healed, his fiancée had been thoroughly depraved by the wait. He succeeded in impregnating her on their wedding night, but not in satisfying her curiosity, as Sforza was ashamed of his slapdash mutilation and refused to let her see or feel. Monsieur Connoisseur died on a bench waiting to rendezvous with a rich Swiss woman who had promised to bring him a manuscript that would make his fortune, and Sforza's mother-in-law moved into the building, the legal owner of the business but content to let Sforza have his head.

After his wife was delivered of her second child—Prosper—she insisted on being converted ritually to her husband's faith to ensure that any further offspring would be Jewish from birth, knowing more now than any Sforza about the subject. Prosper's father rescued a Czech rabbi stranded in Paris after a local boy fluent in French had wooed away his congregation, paying him to come into the maternity ward and do the necessary at her bedside with no questions asked. He congratulated Sforza and sensed no imposture. The police stopped him at the Belgian border and locked him away, returning all his francs to Zeydie Sforza, who by this time had recovered his wits and advertised for the return of his money—which had continued to dwindle as Sforza the Younger's masquerade incurred new expenses. Madame Sforza never bore another child, and the rabbi's relatives assumed he had become too successful to bother keeping in touch.

Prosper's father had the press to himself for five years. He gave it his family's name and expanded its bailiwick to include ribald woodcuts from India, translations of off-color Restoration poetry, and photogravures of female music-hall stars with short biographies and reproductions of their autographs in crimson ink, stamped by hand on every plate and dried by the sugary breath of his little daughter Pasquale. When war seemed inevitable, Sforza gave his wife no peace—despite the risk of opening old wounds—trying to make her pregnant in time to exempt him from conscription. He bought himself a year and a son in this fashion only to see his business flounder in wartime and then fold completely after the late M. Connoisseur's widow discovered her granddaughter reading aloud from the Earl of Rochester's "Signor Dildoe" to a dolly she'd named Theodora. Sforza was taken to court for deceiving the owner of his business and Theodora chucked in the Seine as a synecdoche for sin. Madame Connoisseur emigrated to Quebec; Sforza protested to the magistrate that he was being punished for a deception initiated by his father-in-law, then joined the army to avoid his creditors. His letters from the trenches are masterpieces of both calligraphic technique and urgent, limpid prose; I have thirty mimeographs here from the Holocaust Museum in New York City where the originals were archived, mistakenly, after Prosper Sforza's death. In the end Papa was removed from the front after taking a beating at the hands of his comrades, who caught him pulling a dead German girl in a blue pinafore out of the puddle in which he'd thought she was drowning. (She had already been shot.) They crooked his nose and corrected his childhood malocclusion—too late to miss all but the last six months of fighting.

The youngest Sforza grew up in love with his sister, with whom he never quarreled. She did all she could to avoid him, but with no parents present to complain to and no place to hide, there was nothing to keep toddling Prosper from following her everywhere she went, even into the outhouse and bath. He brought her pebbles from their allotment garden after shining them with his shirt; also wrapping paper he'd found blown into drains, pigeon eggs, and the torn-off lower corners of posters. He'd abide her every tirade and tantrum with sweet, smiling beatitude. Eventually, and not for the last time, the persistence that was second nature to him wore down his target's resolve until she gave up all pretense to privacy or individuation and doted on the little lothario. She even agreed to marry him when he was old enough to support her, and to help him find a way to get them both back onto the floating island Zeydie Sforza had toppled from, back in the last century, when they'd used wax for false noses and not celluloid.

He turned sixteen in 1930. No part of Pasquale's body remained a mystery. He shifted his attentions to a fourteen-year-old neighbor whom he thought would let him fuck her if he showed her the unbound back stock of his father's old company, dusty in a closet on the third floor, since refurbished and rented out as flats. He found it quite impossible to relax in the company of a pretty woman he'd never touched. His discomfort in such situations made him petulant and fidgety, and he had no sympathy for other boys' anxieties regarding the opposite sex. He found his schoolmates backward and preposterous and never hesitated to tell them what was what. Pasquale in the meantime had come through a crippling depression obsessed with having children and leaving France forever. She found and married a vacationing Canadian banker and went to hunt for her maternal grandmother in the New World.

Monsieur and Madame Sforza never guessed that their son was behind Pasquale's flight. They found him inscrutable and glib. Heartbroken, they decided to sell their building and use the money to travel. They settled in Modena and were shunned for being Jewish until World War II, when they were murdered for it. Prosper extorted a small sum from them before they left and did some traveling of his own. He walked and rode through Eastern and Northeastern Europe, repeating his surname to farmers and town registrars in Poland and East Prussia, trying to track down Zeydie Sforza's place of birth. Eventually Prosper was forced to admit defeat. Bereft of other enthusiasms or interests, and frightened of what might be asked of him if he were to return to Paris and enter university, he resolved to drop off the face of the Earth. He settled in a township in Estonia tiny enough to escape the notice of any cartographer born west of the Danube. Content with a life of dirt and blood, gossip, manure, and provincial pussy, he read Longfellow and broke up marriages.

World War II arrives then like astigmatism and we lose Prosper
Sforza for six years. I have here a sham British passport with his
photograph. He has no military record.

When he reappears he's been married and divorced and stories
of his tragic wartime love for a beautiful and pitiless harpy have
been incorporated into his patter. He has money, goes to Modena
to have small monuments built in honor of his parents. He's surprised to find that not a single native remembers them, and begins
to doubt that they'd ever been there. At a poker game he meets
two de-mobbed fascista cinéastes—lieutenants—bemoaning the
near-annihilation of the Italian film industry and jealous that
France had managed to turn out masterpieces even during the
Occupation. There and then Prosper commits his tomb-money
and more to starting a production company with his new friends,
incidentally saving both from execution by the Partisans by involving them in a profitable, high-profile business enterprise before their warrants could be signed.

Prosper's twelfth film (and Evelyn Nevers's third), *La Bocca
del Cavallo* (*The Scarlet Prize*), was a conflation of the legends of
the Trojan War and the Lady Messalina, in which Helen herself
opens the gates of Troy to the Greeks, having exhausted every
gallant within its walls during her week-and-a-half stay. The
movie wrapped and went out to theaters without a hitch, but
Sforza soon found himself distressed. In order to compete in the
world market, his pictures were becoming more explicit every
year. Pornography upset him. He only enjoyed his business when
he could think of himself as showing beautiful naked women to
people who would not ordinarily have had a chance to see them.
He also liked the idea of poking gentle fun at sex, the great ani-
mating force of his life (and what everyone else was really after

anyway, surely). He was just a curtain-puller at the raciest follies in town. Pornography should be stamped out. It made him want to cry. Women making their living that way, fucking strangers on film. The humiliation of it. The squalor. How was it different than prostitution? Could you even call it living? If he'd had the money he would've built a great big mansion for them all to live and rehabilitate in. He'd gather and protect them. But he was barely scraping by. His Italian partners told lies about him to the women on the set so they'd keep their distance. They wanted to edge him out, he figured, and take his house and take his stars and get him sent to a concentration camp (he knew that these were still being run, they'd just been moved underground; how else to explain the stench that came out of his radiator? were they venting the ovens through his gas pipes? was the whole city being heated by burning Jews? Scratch an inch in the soil and Hell was there waiting).

He flew to England, as he always did when he felt low. In his hotel room at 3 A.M. he found himself watching a hypnotic short film on television, incoherent and pleasantly soporific, which then played on in his dreams until sunrise—like a succession of sinister Flemish still lifes tacked to the inside of his head. They reminded him of the inventories of victims' possessions the papers had published during the trials at Nuremberg. He called the BBC and asked to have the names of the persons responsible. They assumed it was a legal matter and gave him Selwyn Wexler's home address. He arrived at ten that morning at a row of thin, flat houses built by the Bank of England and knocked at a pink door until Myrna Krause in a damp black rumpled sweater and sheer blue pajama-bottoms opened up, eating cereal with a wooden spoon. Sforza heard music from inside akin to a Bach partita being bowed on elevator cables. He read the sweater, the cereal, and the music and decided that she'd been in the shower: she'd come out and naked put the needle down on some thin-because-cheap disc of hullabaloo she pretends to like and pulled on her pajamas to be halfway decent but got distracted because she's an artistic type and poured milk into her bowl and sat munching until my knocking startled her and she still damp grabbed the first thing to hand to cover herself and answer. She asked if she could help him and he asked for Mister Wexler, thinking she might be his daughter. She asked which Mister Wexler he wanted and Sforza panicked. He wrote his number at the hotel on his business card and left it with her, showing his open palms as he backed down the three stone steps to the road. She closed the door and he chased after his cab, smitten. Surely so lovely an apple had held on for a shepherd in love. He told the concierge to forward his calls to the bar and settled in on red leather, with a view of the door, drinking beer. She was his first American.

Myrna went back to breakfast having decided that Sforza was a salesman. She told Wexlers *père et fils*, who preferred eggs to cereal, that it had been nothing, no one, and only took the card out of her sweater half a day later, out of boredom at her ticket kiosk in the Underground. The card had Sforza's name, phone number, address in Rome, and now where he could be reached in London. Myrna recognized the name. She often went out to the movies alone. There was now a painless rash on her chest where the card had chafed. She had no phone and so had to wait until her shift ended at midnight to tell Wexler that a man in movies had been to see them. He yelled at her for having let him get away and then took her out the next night for a moderately priced Italian dinner at which they drank too much wine and spent every penny he'd made from the television airing. They fell asleep together in the back of the family car, parked on the street, after Wexler had put Myrna's jeans in the glove box and gone down on her, complaining obscurely as she licked his neck some time later that he felt like this massive crustacean.

Myrna made the call. Prosper had by this time summoned Evelyn because he wanted so much to sleep with the little American. He learned the disposition of her and Wexler's partnership, the division of labor. Sforza asked what their plans were and got an earful of John Wilmot, Earl of Rochester, on whom Myrna was writing her thesis at Winnie's instigation. Wexler had told her about the Rose Alley Ambuscade, when thugs purportedly in Rochester's employ surprised John Dryden in a lonely place and beat him with cudgels: the titled author of existential smut assaulting the lowborn Poet Laureate. If they were going to make a movie, a real movie, with actors and a plot and a string orchestra—which they weren't sure they wanted to do—wouldn't this make a good subject? To her surprise, Rochester's work was not unknown to Sforza. He asked to meet with Krause and Wexler as soon as their schedules allowed. Myrna said that she worked nights till the weekend and that the three of them could talk then. Sforza asked her what she did for a living, and really, what station?

The meeting was set for Saturday, Prosper's fifty-fourth birthday. Myrna had telephoned on Wednesday morning; Evelyn answered in bed and passed the receiver to Sforza over a tray of pears and Stilton cheese. Wednesday night he walked down to Myrna's kiosk with champagne, paper cups, and two antique maps of London circa the Great Fire. (One of these was mislaid; it reappeared in a nearby tunnel twenty-five years later, blown onto the window of a train car, and this resulted in the closing of Myrna's

tube station and the rerouting of circa a thousand passengers while
a thorough archeological investigation took place.) The bookstore
at which he had purchased them, where they'd been kept for a century behind two-inch glass along with brittle issues of *Strand* and
Yellow Book, first editions of Dickens, and privately printed and
Englished Huysmans and Ducasse, had sent a runner to the bank
to deposit his check as soon as Sforza was out of earshot. The bank
was obliged to report the transfer of so large a sum from overseas,
and a Whitehall man—an Earl himself, and founding member
of a peerage-only Evelyn Nevers appreciation society—was thus
informed that Sforza the notorious racketeer had returned, and
apparently was not content to remain inconspicuous.

Myrna was alarmed by her suitor's audacity but happy to have
her shift made quicker by his company. She didn't have the heart
to tell him that it was Wexler who was the Restoration nut, and
enthused in her way over how helpful the maps would be in writing the Rochester script. Prosper spoke of Evelyn and his wartime
belle dame sans merci to excite her, Myrna of Selwyn and her college courses to keep Prosper at the proper distance. He asked if he
could join her again the next night and Myrna said sure, why not,
though she knew why not, and didn't tell Wexler about her visita-
tion when she got home. He didn't notice her tipsiness, just played
cards with Wexler Senior until his mother turned out the lights
on them. The next night Prosper tickled her knee and squeezed
her shoulder and brushed her hair away from her eyes. He refilled
her cup when it was empty and was alarmed and excited by her
bitter Martian smell in such close quarters. Her skin was slick and
textured, unblemished, but in no place smooth.

Myrna enjoyed the simplicity of flirting with him. She wondered at herself that she could as easily be with such a man as

with Selwyn—if she *was* with Selwyn. When he took her hand she stopped him and told him what she preferred. He complained that there was no room there in the kiosk, but she said that was just what she liked, no room. He took off his jacket and hiked up his pant legs and felt like an old letch in the subway. She was rubbery and stiff like an appliance and he was appalled when he came while working on her. She sold a token to a woman who didn't notice their game and he thought he'd better use the scene in Evelyn's next movie. The adventure was repeated on Friday; later he'd learn the ink was just then drying on a warrant for his arrest. It made the memory irresistible. He assumed he'd never been happier.

3
Myrna Krause

Already there were disturbances; outside of Paris police were surrounding a university campus built like an industrial park where students had occupied the Dean's office and were walking out on their exams. A woman cuirassed by a sandwich board advertising a stationers' shop in the Latin Quarter backed into Myrna on a corner and insisted on being punished rather than apologize. Myrna went shopping for fountain-pen nibs and a man on a mat playing a zurna on the Boulevard Saint-Michel asked to have one to write to his family, then blew a hoarse flat note on it, cutting his tongue.

It was almost April. The rind of winter ice on the sidewalks became black and slight, its divestiture trickling into the retiform fractures between the cobblestones. Sometimes the nights were sufficiently cold for the seepage to freeze before finding a gutter, leaving the morning streets grosgrained by wrinkly cords that would shatter under her weight. She walked a mile back and forth each day to get to know her new neighborhood and got blistered and propositioned. Winnie wouldn't come along. All he wanted to do was stay in and work on her script. He paced from radiator to radiator like an invalid and took taxis even to the grocery two blocks up. He wore scarves in the bath and wouldn't go to the Tower or Louvre because he was afraid of being mistaken for *un touriste*. She told him about the student demonstrations in the suburbs and he mumbled something about taking the train down to see what it was all about, then changed his mind after she brought him a timetable, saying his lack of French would only make him a liability. You go, he told her. I'll stay here and make short work of this draft. Anyway, it'll be short. Myrna threw away the timetable and walked for the better part of the morning along the Seine until she reached the Tower, which she had heard was the place you went in Paris when you didn't want to see it.

She had been born in Michigan twenty-eight years and seven months previous. When she was twenty-one she received an encouraging rejection letter from the little journal *Locus Solus*, which she showed her parents to convince them to let her out of music school. Her mother Rose was a typist at an insurance company and her father Michael a retired factory worker (car parts). Neither were readers; both were second-generation German-American Methodists; both had been born with stutters that so disfigured their speech that they had as schoolchildren in the same parish learned to communicate with one another by whistling the choruses of popular tunes whose titles contained phrases practical to everyday life; e.g., "What's New," "Betcha Nickel," "Open the Door, Richard," "I Want the Waiter (With the Water)," "What's the Matter with Me?," "Keep Cool, Fool," "Undecided," "Oh, Lady Be Good!," and, eventually, "I Can't Believe that You're in Love with Me."

He proposed with "Who Takes Care of the Caretaker's Daughter"—risky—and she accepted with "'Deed I Do." They were sixteen. They had the notary write letters detailing their intentions and left them stuck with peppermint chewing gum on the iceboxes in each of their homes—they were neighbors—then went to a movie to give their parents time to read and react. Neither expected trouble. It was clear that they were good for each other. Their infrequent efforts at intelligible speech were so gruesome and heartbreaking to behold—with tongues like purple geese molting spittle and phlegm—that simple questions from one or both had at times occasioned debilitating traumas in those who received them. Rose and Michael had already cost the town its minister, sheriff, and schoolteacher, each of whom wept a full day and night before resigning their posts and disappearing.

A marriage was in the public good. When they were together they didn't open their mouths except to pucker. A two-story house closer to the auto works than downtown was purchased with money from the Health and Welfare budget and the couple installed there with a brand new radio that shone green when it was warmed up and got stations from as far away as Tokyo.

Life was quiet until an anthropologist named Pantry and a piano-playing sociologist with a strong left hand moved in for thirteen months when Rose and Michael turned twenty. They wrote a book that no one in town would read, cataloging the vocabulary of over one thousand five hundred ideo-melodic phrases used in the Krause household. Rose and Michael had by this time begun to employ a kind of shorthand: a few bars could be used to signify any of a daunting array of words and phrases, and the Krauses had even begun to *combine* disparate song-snatches to form awkward sentences (and tunes) of their own construction (e.g., a combination of "Some Days There Ain't No Fish" and "Yes! We Have No Bananas" might indicate that there would be fish for dinner). Despite the potential for expressive nicety this method might indicate, the scientists observed that the Krauses did not have conversations as we understand them: the sense of their short whistles consisted in the main of questions, answers, and reassurances regarding continued love or fidelity, this last accompanied by one's pinching the earlobe or index finger of the other. Thus, the ingenuity they had displayed in assembling and fine-tuning their makeshift language was in the service of modulation rather than an expanded eloquence. They went about their lives independently, with the radio on, and usually didn't deign to "speak." When circumstances made the articulation of a new concept necessary, a period of intense study was initiated, with Rose or Michael begging off work and attending the wireless for hours at a time: grimly perusing their makeshift dictionary with only a definition in hand, searching for the corresponding word. Due to a dearth (then as now) of songs dealing with pregnancy, and the couple's obstinate refusal to communicate with one another via writing, Rose spent weeks tuned in before settling on Artie Shaw's rendition of "There's Something in the Air"—quite abstract—with which she then had to acquaint her husband by means of a trip to the music shop, and further clarify with suggestive motions, before he understood that he was to be a father. When the two academics took their leave they pooled their resources and purchased the Krauses a record player, promising to return in ten years time to inspect their sure-to-be extraordinary offspring.

Bebop and Myrna bewildered them. Even lips and tongues as pronounced as the Krauses' were incapable of keeping every

note of a bop record differentiated at the necessary tempi, and
if they couldn't imitate it, they couldn't hear it. (The exception
being Thelonious Monk's "Well, You Needn't," which Myrna ordered from the general store when she was an antinomian ten.
Though they considered it three steps from anarchy, it was too
catchy a tune and too useful a title to ignore. They'd never before
had access to such artful contempt.) When, after meeting Prosper
Sforza, Myrna wrote from England to tell them that she would
be going to Paris for a year, their only response was to inquire
whether this was the city where, on Louis Armstrong's first visit,
men had absconded with his trumpet and disassembled it under
bright lights, looking to isolate his secret. Neither the Krauses
nor the French understood that a language is obliged to accept
heterogeneous elements in order to survive.

She was never a crier. Baby Myrna was inured to histrionics almost from birth by her parents' well-intentioned soliloquies over
her cradle. Her grandparents—a dangerous, hardy, and sagacious
quartet of literate lower-class Rhinelanders—intervened when she
began imitating their hobbled speech and attaching semantic significance to every sputter and false start. Rose and Michael gave
up verbalization forever, without regret, while their parents made
it their business to teach Myrna some proper English. They visited
and read to her from newspapers; they took her away on weekends
and threw dinner parties so that she'd be surrounded by chatter.
Talk was Myrna's castor oil: they forced it down her throat. She
grew up hating them and their prattle and considered the spoken
word unseemly. She carried into her twenties the conviction that
articulate speech was a demeaning biological obligation, along
the lines of an excretion. She taught herself to read in order to
save herself from confinement at those daily recitations from the

New York Times or *Life*, and soon found the smudged lineaments of newsprint very pretty . . . prettier, certainly, than any voice.

She was made to attend school from age five, but didn't speak a word in class until the teacher swatted her with a yardstick after a particularly petulant silence was perceived to have ruined morning prayers. At our interview in Manhattan she pulled back her wig and showed me where, she said, the blow had landed: a slight concavity of the skull, not unusual in infants born to rural communities before 1960: the work of some ham-handed country doctor who probably plunked her in a dish of white vinegar and parsley after her feet came free of mom. I told her what it looked like to me and asked did she really believe her story. She said William Carlos Williams himself had delivered her as he passed through Michigan on a lecture tour. I asked her when she'd got so full of shit and she made me promise to tell the elevator operator not to let me back in when I left. I gave my word and kept it.

Newspapers took to running stories on cargo cults, jungle tribes that had attached religious significance to the white men come with fantastical gifts during the war and waiting now for their return, compulsively building and abandoning landing strips, as the Mayans did their cities. The anthropologist remembered his promise. He arrived at the back door of the house and told the Krauses over dinner how the boogie-woogie sociologist was shot dead escaping from a camp where he'd been detained after his arrest for desertion. Myrna was twelve and in shorts and an inveterate masturbator. As the anthropologist talked about his wartime experiences in the Congo among natives who transmitted detailed messages over miles of veldt through chains of trained whistlers hidden in the high grass, she moved her pelvis imperceptibly along the rounded wooden northwest corner of her chair. Pantry said that he hoped Myrna would prove to be a great composer or instrumentalist, having been born into such a musical family. He alone noticed her squirming, but attributed it to boredom and possibly a native sense of rhythm.

With mortgage and grant money he paid for a second-hand Steinway and lessons under a not-too-famous émigré lately resident in Traverse City who had no memory of playing for the Czar at the age of twelve. He arrived the first day in a fur coat and presented the Krauses with a plump pearl metronome from his collection. Pantry refused to admit defeat when the girl's short, broad fingers daunted her prospective instructor and her listlessness at the keyboard all but provoked the aging prodigy to violence. Rose made up a room for Pantry in the attic and no one but Myrna wondered when he'd be leaving.

He was an insomniac. She heard him walking above her at night, later than she'd ever been awake, making her ceiling rasp and snap like a rocking chair. At first she could sleep regardless, exhausted by her music lessons, which followed her dismissal from school at three o'clock and ran until dinner. As summer came on, school was closed, and the days lengthened, she found it more difficult. The weather was unbearable that year; she lay awake on her blanketless bed, sweating, spread-eagled, arms and legs straining away from the heat of her trunk. The piano needed tuning every morning, and a plague of millipedes fell on the Krauses—so thin, dry, and brittle that they threatened to combust in the swelter, squiggling autographs in fire, and start the whole house burning. The air in the attic was impossible to breathe, but Pantry wouldn't move down to the living-room sofa. He said the jungle was worse: like living in a vegetable steamer. The books he'd brought had turned into blank pulp—little brittle bricks that he'd abandoned and by now become beige soil. The dye had come out of his clothing and stained him while he slept. The silt in his pores had cooked and caked like crystals on his skin. He thought his eyes might swim out if he turned his head too quickly. No, the attic was a breeze.

Myrna took to playing with herself to pass the slow, sludgy hours between her bedtime and her father's leaving for work at six. She lost weight and caught every cold that passed through town. She fell asleep at the piano and everyone worried that her instructor would murder her. The nights were long and she wasn't allowed to read in bed. She lost what little capacity for enjoyment she had, while Pantry, for his part, never showed the slightest wear. Myrna wondered how he'd learned to go without sleep. Was it some secret he'd picked up in the jungle? Or was it that his dreams were so appalling that he was grateful to pace?

She worried it would go on all summer. She thought of throwing herself in the lake, or into some machine at the factory, until a solution finally presented itself. On a night her ministrations were proving particularly florid, she fetched a sigh that managed to reach Pantry's ears in the attic, directly above. He froze, as did Myrna in her bed. Soon she heard him get on his knees and put his ear to the floor. He waited an hour, listening, before resuming his rounds. Myrna marveled: one little sound had made an hour of silence. Could the anthropologist be persuaded to listen all night?

She learned to get her sleep in a series of twelve forty-five minute naps, waking near the hour to make noises (sham or genuine, as her temperament dictated) of the sort that seemed to have caught the anthropologist's fancy. Heretofore her self-abuse had been empty of erotic significance, hermetic and self-centered, a

naïve discovery. Now Pantry had taught her that other people
could be persuaded to take an interest—and that their interest
might even surpass her own. Pantry's manifested itself as a kind
of religious horror; it didn't take much to make him ashamed. As
a child in Wales he had been Myrna's perfect opposite: loud and
chaste, presumptuous and filthy. He shopped his anodyne and bewildered parents as kidnappers the summer of his sixth year, when
his hair had turned a bright Hibernian red, and refused after def-
ecation to clean himself unaided until he was twelve years old.

At boarding school he fell in love. He withdrew and became
fat and afraid and repentant. Habitually guilty people are most at
ease when they have something specific and appalling to regret:
Pantry had spent his life carefully engineering opportunities to
localize this otherwise unfocused distress. Having entered into
what he considered an unspeakable pact with an adolescent (whose
complicity he saw evidenced in her every word and gesture, when
he wasn't dismissing it as monstrous, or—anyway—unlikely),
Pantry was free to lose interest in Myrna's welfare and potential
as a musical prodigy and concentrate instead on fretting over the
many professional and romantic disappointments that had twice
deposited him in rural Michigan when his place was in the jungle,
a martyr to the study of man, to be depicted in stained-glass faith-
fulness on the back of a sleeping Negro boy.

Only now did he come down to breakfast worn and withdrawn.
He stopped asking Myrna about her music and stopped attending her lessons, stopped looking her in the eye and squeezing her
shoulder and began taking his dinner in the attic. She misunder-
stood his new egocentrism as censure, and, having metabolized
a little of his shame, began to apply herself to music as though
it really interested her. She started collaging other composers'

works—easy pieces kept in the piano bench—stealing simple runs she could hear in her head without having to play them and transposing the sequences backward or diagonally across her staff paper, like a crossword puzzle without the black bars, until it was a gibberish of conflicting methods. Then, in her best hand, which was delightfully precise, she'd iron out the inconsistencies and delete the incompatibilities until she found a motif worth repeating. She'd repeat it three times, twice before and once after a new phrase in a different tempo, like a pop song. She assembled lyrics from newspaper articles—crimes of passion held her interest best—making lists of words with the right number of syllables for her melodies and putting them together in clusters that could suggest a simple "Frankie and Johnny"–type story without any added prepositions, then slipped the finished miniatures under Pantry's door, two or three an afternoon. He collected them unread in his trunk for a week and finally gave the songs to Myrna's music teacher. The unhappy man accused the girl of making fun of him and slapped her so that her cheek stood out blue and pink. He then wept into the open Steinway, rubbing his fingers along the wire, calling a dead woman's name, chopped incoherent by the vibrato.

Big Michael Krause took the maestro out of the piano and put his thumbs into the Russian's Adam's apple. After Pantry and Rose separated the two, and the extended family sulked over lemonade in the kitchen, the teacher put his pearl metronome into a green baize box and left the house for good, promising with what remained of his voice that he'd get Myrna a scholarship to Julliard if and when she wanted, but not to contact him until.

She hated it there. The men were tired and the women treacly; nobody called after the third date. She had a loft in a commer-

cial building in sight of Lincoln Center and still couldn't play the
piano.

She had by this time written three operettas, score and libretto
both, without composing a single note; had even managed to get
part of one played and sung by other students during a disastrous
parents' night. It was an adaptation of a play called *Sodom*, falsely
attributed to John Wilmot, a copy of which—printed for subscrib-
ers in 1901 and festooned with pornographic woodcuts—she'd acquired for five dollars from a cart in Washington Square. Pantry
flew in to see it and got chest pains when Myrna gave him a blow-
job in his hotel room after the show. He gave her a signed copy
of his book on her parents and disappeared, ostensibly to take a
professorship at Oxford. The girl felt a curious relief after tasting
Pantry and stopped going to class. She submitted her text pieces
as poems to local literary journals and received some trivial ap-
probation for a jagged and top-heavy Rochester jabberwocky that
made most editors blush to their ears.

She decided to go after Pantry and apply to read English
Literature. He pulled strings for her but refused to meet; he was
employed dusting display cases in the natural history museum,
but was still in touch with a few masters, provosts, and wardens
from their days together at public school, and was owed a number of favors. She never knew he was dying a few blocks away
while she was in Paris with Wexler, whom she met at a lecture on
Andrew Marvell, one face in two hundred. He wrote trenchant
film reviews for the student paper, was the rudest person she'd
ever known, and was an expert on her pet poet, who till now she'd
thought was her own discovery. Wexler and she began meeting
and drinking beer after hours in the high-ceilinged apartment he
shared with two other boys, and he told her late into Christmas

morning that she looked like something that hadn't been finished. He always managed to avoid consummating their amore by one excuse or another—once even after penetration—and left her in such a state that she fell into bed with both of his flatmates during the winter vacation (severally, mind you, and quite by accident), precipitating a fair amount of bloodshed. Selwyn used a letter-opener to puncture the anterior tibial artery of the house Pre-Raphaelite, while the boy was kicking him earnestly in the stomach and chest with his free foot. The last in line, Chaucer, who had no complaints, phoned the authorities and an ambulance. Pre on the stretcher complained that he felt like his wounded leg had been sucked into smoldering quicksand. Staunched, he swore revenge.

Myrna and Selwyn went to London. His parents made a guest room for her on the ground floor in a space that doubled as a second cold-cellar for vegetables and beer. The students never shared a bed and neither went back north for the spring term; Selwyn referred to this hiatus as their "rustication" and his craggy parents began to fret. Retired professors, they were astonished that Myrna had been allowed into Oxford; they suggested she might be happier among her own kind. The Wexlers had been middle-aged when Selwyn was conceived and were determined to see him settled before they climbed into the twin cemetery plots they'd purchased when he was still a toddler, so as to avoid inconveniencing him when the time came to have them buried—he was three years older than Myrna and finishing his thesis on the Rose Alley Ambuscade; he had far more to lose than his American bint and so ought to stop being foolish. He didn't defend her, but declaimed, *Kiss me thou curious miniature of man! How odd thou art! how pretty! how japan! Oh, I could live and die with thee!*, later, in private.

When she got back from the Tower she painted his heels with feather-green ink. The lines in his skin stayed pink, however, and he woke from his nap before she could get back with a fine-bristle lettering brush. To be able to purchase such things after dark was the sign of a great civilization, she said. What animal do you think these hairs come from? And would a primate's do as well?

4
Abelard Pantry

Each panel of this hinged silver-print triptych of the Pantries of Pembrokeshire, 1892, has been meringued with corrections and embellishments by hand. The lusterless halftones camouflage flaws but dull the sharpness of the images, serving to bring them into alignment with the then-contemporary taste for fuzzy mezzotint reproductions of old masters. In this case, you'll note, the photographer has done more than tincture hair and clothes. Two-year-old Abelard is the most affected. He insisted on staring into the flash, so new eyes had to be painted to blot the boy's wrinkled cheeks and slitted lids. Settling the bill, Fulbert Pantry complained that his son fair looked like he caught two tea saucers full in the face. To me they look less definite than crockery—doughier. They eclipse his head and leak into the air like sculpture. But those giggling travesties are the only eyes you'll find on Abelard anywhere in my files. The new century's vogue for verisimilitude made such prettifying déclassé, so posterity is free to see him wincing in every shot—in every goddamn photograph from age two to seventy-eight—as though continually posed in line with the sun.

Noontime light falls on Pantry's forehead in this, his last photo—postmortem in fact—in April and in Paris. Innocent of his subject's demise, the photographer asked the old man to try and relax. The shutter twitched with a civilized tick and the picture taker wound fastidiously to his next frame. Pantry was still. Still squinting. He held the scruff of his trouser legs by the knees. By the time his friend tried to wake him, there was a very red and dusty sunset coming through their window. If there had been any juice left in his brain, Pantry probably would have thought it looked like Africa.

Thirty years earlier we have a professional-looking shot of him among Bushmen in the Kalahari. He's in muslin; they're in skin aprons and sandals. The date-stamp is red and was checkered by somebody's thumb. The natives look practiced and attractive, like they've been posing all their lives. One is glowering with crossed arms and chin put forward; another is candid, his hands folded behind his head, watching something over your shoulder; both as though they're in an ad. Only Pantry is awkward; he ruins the shot: looks nervous, burnt, and constipated. Perhaps he'd had a premonition. A massacre perpetrated by Boer out to secure the mining rights to certain tribal hunting grounds ended his stay prematurely; he was sent by the headman to start criminal proceedings in Pretoria but at the first opportunity stole off to London instead.

And here's a school photo. A round one hundred boys, out of one hundred four: three absented by whooping cough and one drowned. Under a magnifying glass we can make out Abelard's baby-face, twisted to a point like stirred pudding. Next to him a blond boy who looks fresh from the foam at Cyprus. The boys were meant to be positioned by surname, but this one's a bee among the peas. And is Pantry holding his hand? Blondie is lopsided like a buoy.

Ask a photographer: if you take a picture of a religious man, have you made a religious picture? Mr. Fulbert Pantry went to Mass each morning, trained racehorses, and was aggressively scrutinized by his Presbyterian neighbors for the unusual comfort in which he kept his family. Fulbert made winners: a beast called Salt Water was his bread and butter. He was proud and strong and short and went about naked before 10 A.M. and after five in the evening, his member looking like some hypertrophied overnight toadstool to tiny Abelard, who often dug these up from the meadows by the cathedral.

Fulbert's proclivity—predating the advent of contemporary nudism, predicated by the publication in 1906 of Richard Ungewitter's *Die Nacktheit*—was neither shared nor sanctioned by Dolores, his wife, who blamed this perversion on a life in the stables, and was itself Fulbert's only bow to iconoclasm in a life otherwise calcified by convention. He found and collected arguments obliquely supporting his predilection from the newspapers, copied them into his commonplace book, and then brought them up as though by chance at the dinner table, when Dolores couldn't escape—William and Catherine Blake in their garden being a favorite, despite the mad poet's anticlericalism; the longing for prelapsarian grace; the purity and simplicity of equatorial savages living in states of nature, rising with the sun on their skin, sleeping at dusk, too tired for psychology, cooled by winds freely flowing, etc. Dolores was never convinced—was inconvincible—but she listened and remembered. She was compiling evidence. She spent all her time with Master Abelard, and was the first to notice his peculiarities. It was clear from whence they came.

I have copies of his birth certificate and school enrollment forms. His eyes started out brown but later resolved to blue, just as his hair one day became a shock of red. A nanny threw herself pregnant into the Alun River when he was six—about the time G. B. Shaw was getting married, Eugene Atget started photographing Paris, and Aubrey Vincent Beardsley was dying of tuberculosis in Menton, having just received a commission to illustrate Lord Rochester's poem "The Imperfect Enjoyment" for a private edition—and Dolores told Abelard it was all because he'd forced the girl to wipe his bottom. Now he decided that Fulbert and Dolores were so unmistakably a picture of barrenness that he must have been the child of good Puritan bricklayers from the North Country, snuck from his bassinet to help the popish Pantries put up a plausible public front of fecundity. His hair was Queen's Evidence: it put Dolores and Fulbert in the dock for a week while his real parents were sought, according to the boy's detailed description, and Abelard slept on goose-down at the Sergeant's house, waiting to be claimed. The Pantry lawn wilted, and the presbyters put threatening letters into their mailbox. Dolores became convinced she'd caught scabies in jail and, even after the cure, continued to scratch and complain. Salt Water broke a leg being exercised by a stranger and had to be put down. Fulbert spent his first night free away from home, naked on the gelding's hay.

Until he was well into university, Abelard believed that Freud was the name of a bald, vulture-winged boogeyman who swooped down on little boys and girls naughty enough to peek at each others' privates and spirited them off to burn forever in Austria—the invention of a thickly Welsh and possibly schizoid Sunday school instructor. Thus, he felt no self-consciousness whatever at finding himself drawn, by and by, to both kiss and trowel out the paternal genitals so often on display. Fulbert cursed and drank and smelled like turned earth; Abelard loathed him for his chthonic dullness but found him deafeningly lovely. Father was unnerved. He realized with a start that his boy was teaching him how to be ashamed.

He'd hated his own dad, of course—a phlegmatic dockworker whose ambitions had extended no farther than snooker and a hobby fashioning elaborate novelty watch faces. He hadn't even invited the coot to his wedding. So Fulbert had been prepared for child rearing to be a battle. He didn't even mind, really, that Abelard wore the pants in the family. The boy would sort himself out. Time would see to it. He'd be respectable—a Pantry at Oxford. If not, well, he'd think better of it when they beat his teeth down his throat with pumice stones at school. No one likes a monster.

But this, now, wasn't the sanctified, wholesome, historical distaste Fulbert had been looking forward to. Abelard's staring made him feel exposed. Delicate too. Though in truth the boy was still largely ignorant of sex, and rather slow to even conceive of such a thing, Fulbert couldn't help but bring his age and experience to bear in interpreting his son's steady gawking. F's oft-used commonplace book goes blank for two months following his record of moneys spent on a day-trip to the track and stables with Abelard (Dolores's idea, a stab at easing tensions). What happened there is a mystery—jockeys are short-lived and gamblers incognito—but Fulbert's response was decisive; the next entry tells us that the Pantries sold their house and took Abelard to the Jesuits, a full year early. They gave him two pounds and told him to write them every day, copying down their new address for him with two digits transposed, by accident or design.

It was a small and very modern school. First thing, they gave him a physical: bled him into a cylinder with one end tapered like a bullet and the other made to take a dainty cork the size and shape of your thumb. Abelard wondered what kind of man would invent a receptacle he could never safely set down. The old woman who'd stuck him opened a great metal icebox that shimmied on its base of three Indian rubber stops and one scrunched *Summa* of Aquinas. The thickening blood of one hundred three boys swayed inside, each in the grip of its own metal pincer, but lightly, looking liable to fall. An older boy led him by the tie to the dormitory, empty at that time of day, but still a shock to Abelard, who couldn't imagine anything but a fleet of Pullman cars being kept in so cavernous a space, and who proceeded to wet his pants and forget to keep the wad of cotton pressed against his wound. Bloody now and smelling properly fit-in, he was taken by a growing crowd of between-class boys to the newly installed lavatory, which reminded him of a horse trough, containing as it did for liquid waste a basin ten yards long and two feet wide, faucet at its left end and drain at its right, made for elbow-to-elbow republican pissing. More substantial excretions still had to be executed in the forest of midget outhouses by the rugby field, and were permitted only once a day, after sport. Sure that they intended to strip him and straight away perform some horrible rite, Abelard frustrated his guides by jumping into the trough and stamping the dirty water there into the air, making the other boys moan and step away from the splash, marveling at his superior filthiness. He screamed obscenities at them loudly enough to get Father Healy up from the refectory to beat the holy hell out of him. Naked now, his soiled Sunday clothes put in the incinerator to go the way of Salt Water, Abelard was plunked back into sick bay and left to shiver. Soon the matron brought a companion, in blue uniform and cap, everything but his tie a size too large and skin braided ear to toe with chicken pox. Matron took the pariah's temperature before clearing out to arrange his quarantine.

Abelard in his disgrace was happy to see there was a child at school younger and more desolate than he. The littler boy was reading Sir E. A. Wallis Budge's translation of the Egyptian *Book of the Dead*. Abelard wished aloud he'd thought to bring a book and then complained that he would get infected. He told the boy to sit farther away, but the interloper wouldn't budge. Abelard wanted to hit him, but the boy was, in a sense, inviolate. How could he be hurt without one's handling his pollution?

Abelard asked his name, but the boy shook his blond head no. Abelard asked was he shy. Maybe he liked to be coaxed. Blondie replied out of the side of his mouth that he did, just don't *you* coax me. Abelard made an obscene noise and then was inspired. He told Blondie that he was just tall enough to reach the blood cabinet and steal Blondie's vial; it would give Abelard power over him, like a witch doctor who with a bag of nail and hair clippings could cause his well-groomed enemies to sicken and expire.

Blondie's interest was piqued. He peered nastily over his Budge, as though aware that his tormentor would grow up to meet sorcerers galore, that many would pronounce him an excellent candidate for the profession and even offer to write him letters of recommendation on the stretched eyelids of their long-dead rivals. Blondie said that his name was Beltham but that he was only saying so in order for Pantry to find the right capsule. Abelard stood on his chair and its sterilized rubber cushion and took the loose corrugated padlock off of its hook, goose pimpled all over. He dropped the thing to the floor, where it didn't bounce, and Beltham, watching, threw his head sideways—to an unfeasibly right angle, reminding Abelard of a jockey he'd seen killed by a fall—stretching his neck until at last it made a noise like logs burping in the hearth. At this signal Abelard blushed and got an erection, which had occurred only rarely to this point, and then with much discomfort and no apparent stimulus—something like a migraine. Innocent of its connotations, the boy was more embarrassed by his coloring, and he rummaged through the cold cabinet violently to hide his distress, losing feeling in his fingers. Four capsules disturbed by his elbows fell to the bottom of the cabinet with a particular clunk, then rolled with nauseous feints and wobbles into space. One shattered near the padlock, its cargo clotting on contact with oxygen, while three landed safe on Abelard's cushion: a deeper shade of red now that they'd been well mixed.

Pantry couldn't have been more pleased that the school's staple punishment was a month locked in the cellar, alone every night and for every meal. Matron would send down a cold plate with Father Healy and every night the priest inquired as to Abelard's respiration, concerned over the damp, then sat and read to the boy from his contraband copy of De Quincy's *Confessions* as long as he thought seemly. During Abelard's few hours aboveground, he made a point of complaining to his classmates about the cellar's swampy atmosphere and the moldering hymnals stored there, nests now for superannuated beetles that struggled out every night, vibrating by his ears and open lips like gray milkweed pods gripped by hummingbirds. He prayed every morning nonetheless that the rector would think of a reason to prolong his sentence.

Abelard spent his birthday in the cellar. Healy came with cake and told him that Gilbert Beltham's was only days away: Lady Beltham herself was coming from Switzerland to collect her son for a weeklong outing through France and thence to the family house in Berne. If Healy had known how much the little aristocrat had been on Abelard's mind during his confinement, he wouldn't have let go this information so casually. Abelard piled fifty or sixty of his book-nests that night under a rectangular crank-operated window and stood on them to crawl out. He began to sink, and had to hoist himself onto the ledge with only the strength of his two arms, as the books, compressing like peat moss underneath him and exhaling a breath of brittle wing remnants, gave no purchase. The grass was wet and cold but cleaner feeling to bare feet than the hymnals, and Abelard skirted around the main building to the infirmary where he had spent so much of his first day at school. He was surprised to find Matron still awake, or at least at large, filling her armchair, drowsing, swiveled to face the open door with a George Sand split on her lap and a cup of fresh peppermint tea steeping on the edge of her examination table, where she must have set it before sitting down. She had only a maritime oil lamp to read by, and as Abelard padded through the room his sleepy eyes saw the steam reaching from her tea as a white cat crouched on the counter beneath the blood-cupboard. By the time he reread the scene correctly, his heart was beating so loudly that he couldn't judge how much noise his feet were making on the tile.

Beltham, who had since recovered, woke up in the dormitory the next morning between Bellwether weeping and Bishop with his blanket twisted between his legs to find Abelard's capsule sweating under his pillow like an icicle. Papers further to an in-

complete memoir, forwarded to me by the Waldau Clinic, where
Beltham was to be confined for much of his later life, tell us that
young Gilbert was, remarkably, able to interpret this gesture successfully as being an awkward, even poignant, declaration on
Pantry's part. Beltham also recalls, in his notes, that it was around
this time, looking into the tiny silver mirror set in the upper lid
of his pocket watch—a gift from Lady Beltham, who had felt terrible guilt after sending Gilbert away to school, and a novelty
whose mechanism and numbering were reversed, readable only in
reflection—that he saw a remarkable blue light emitting from the
center of his forehead, like a gaslight's behind a keyhole, as though
he were some radiant Oriental god gone incognito in short pants
and blazer. No one else seemed to notice, or dared to comment,
but Pantry had the most peculiar way of *staring*. Yes, Abelard saw
it all right, Beltham wrote in his dotage, but the boy was a little
bashful—overawed.

Thus Pantry gawked his way into Beltham's good graces. The
rector authorized his emancipation, at Lady Beltham's special request, pending Fulbert and Dolores's approval of course, though
no response was forthcoming to Lady Beltham's telegram; and
when it became clear that waiting any longer might make them
miss their train, she shrugged and said they'd try again from
home. She was taking the boy up, out of kindness; what possible
objection could the Pantries have?

Abelard got his first sight of London: sooty, chilly station-backs
and chestnut-hawkers like murderers made mute by his window's
thickness and the shrill steam whistles, the guttering of wheel on
track and the anxiety of his fellow passengers pushing one another out into the air. When mother, son, and guest in Calais set-

tled into the private car Lady Beltham had rented—every cranny seeded with tiny gold-ribboned sachets of lavender—she ordered a light supper without first consulting the menu, then set about trying to get Abelard talking by asking what he thought about reincarnation—that is, dear, that we've all lived several times. Abelard wasn't familiar with the concept and replied that he'd always been alive, as far as he could tell, and that he didn't think he would brook any gaps in the current. Gilbert scowled, but Lady Beltham was tickled, and explained to Abelard that Gilbert was thought to have lived many lives previous to this, according to her spiritualist: that his was a most important soul—or *souls*, the boy interrupted, proceeding to embark on a lengthy account of his latest readings in Oriental eschatology.

She was quite young to be a mother, and was the only woman Abelard had ever seen smoke a cigarette or wear trousers, though to please her son she confined herself to snuff and covered her legs with a tartan-colored rug on the train. She put a pinch up her nose after meals and whenever there was a stop too brief to properly stretch one's legs outside, ignoring the children's incessant requests for permission to play in the snow or chitchat with the walrusy conductor.

She didn't much mind when Abelard declared imperiously that Gilbert should kiss him on the lips whenever the train went through a tunnel, with the rationalization following that Dolores used to do the same, to calm him as an infant afraid of the dark, since Lady Beltham was an anarchist at heart. She even suggested that the boys use their tongues, remarking that it would be most appropriate given the country they were traveling through, then spoke about how odd she used to find it that the French word for frank, as in forthright, had the same root as the English, *franche-ment*, implying on the face of it that both cultures attached an ethnogeographic significance to candor. But the word came from the Latin *Francus*: when the Romans occupied Gaul, only the native Franks remained free, and so their name became equated with liberty, and thus the right to be startlingly direct. Still, in the same vein, she had heard the word "English" used lately in terms of topspin, or billiard "side," in several languages, including English, and whence then did this usage originate, and what did it signify that Anglophones accepted it?

She went on to wonder why it was that one feels thirst in the mouth but hunger in the stomach, and soon Gilbert informed her rudely that neither boy found her the least bit interesting. Abelard apologized for his friend when the latter went out to find the facilities, and years later Lady Beltham got him a scholarship to Wadham College, even corresponding with him when he went abroad. Gilbert attended Wadham too, for medicine, and the two went around together for old times' sake, long enough for Abelard to lose his virginity, make friends in society, and secure them both a place on an upcoming royal archeological expedition to the Sinai Peninsula. Before they sailed, however, Gilbert was expelled for striking his tutor and left England in disgrace, without so much as a letter. Abelard broke into Gilbert's rooms to read his papers but found that most had already been sautéed on a hotplate with some celery stalks and made into a salty paste; what remained legible led him to believe that Gilbert had for the past six months been courting a pregnant Oxford laundress named Beth, and so Abelard determined to drown himself by leaping from his steamship somewhere between Plymouth and Palestine.

In the end, seasickness prevented him from leaving his cabin, so

he had a blameless Arab serving-boy put ashore for theft instead.
Brought aft in a sedan chair, Pantry watched through field glasses
as the dejected child scouting the beach receded and bleached in
the mist. There now, Abelard said to a colleague. He can just stay
there and think about what he's done.

5
Gilbert Beltham

There is ghostly footage from Cannes on the television as decrepit villain Gilbert Beltham waits in his high altitude chalet to be allowed back into France, at the behest of his supporters—the many bickering groupuscules united in incessant roundelay along the ancient, prescribed route for Parisian demonstrations: across the river, to the Arc de Triomphe, along to the Place de la Bastille, and back to the Latin Quarter, passing the Grand Palais and Assemblée Nationale on the way—that mile-long serpent with a loudspeaker cone for a head. Gilbert got terrible reception, but he thought he saw Godard put his pipe-stem so far up a journalist's nose that the bourgeois blew blood and vegetable gristle through the bowl; while Polanski, withdrawing *Rosemary's Baby* from competition, did an obscene Polish belly dance before the newsreel cameras, gyrating right off the podium and into the air, a whirligig of satanic energy, before disappearing through the roof like a ghost, vibrating so quickly now that his atoms and those of the ceiling passed each other by like soap bubbles in a bathing beauty

phantasmagoria. Truffaut translated these gestures for the lay-
man: the directors were shutting down the festival in solidarity
with the students and workers of France. The doors and windows
of the auditorium were locked and the press conference turned
into an impromptu colloquium on the formation of an interna-
tional revolutionary cinema. It was all going according to plan.

But certain people—Gilbert could never understand why—
were still immune to his power. It wasn't due to an indomitable resolve or high degree of intelligence; his nurse Danielle was proof
of that. He couldn't get through to her. She came regularly to
dust with her very French feather duster, pert as though newly
plucked, on tiptoe and pubescent as any of the pretty black and
white domestics he had fondled as an adolescent. Or she would
bring him lunch, a new ream of paper, or just come to chat when
she was feeling lazy and didn't want to continue with her rounds,
when she would do leg-bends on the windowsill, having rolled up
her ankle-length dress, letting him see the backs of her thighs and
the institutional blue garters the girls wore there at the clinic.

She wouldn't even read to him, let alone unbutton her top and
let him warm his withered hands under her arms. Prometheus on
the rock got more mercy from his vultures—at least he was left on
his own at night—whereas Danielle, smelling of wine and mucous,
with lips still pink from a dinnertime date, would sneak in even in
the wee hours to check Gilbert's bedpan and temperature, or else
flip him over (he was light as a pencil) to knife him in the ass with
a needle long as a zebra's prick, without so much as a warning.
He watched her as she made small talk, hiding in his room from
her supervisor, parroting her Flemish fiancé's blather about the
strikes, or else asking without interest about Gilbert's past—his
time in the Great War, his breakfast with Erich von Stroheim,

whether his mother as a young widow had really been courted by
Apollinaire and that troglodyte Debussy both—and he knew as he
stared that his eyes were like bonfires on his face, flaring through
the eyeholes in his black half-mask under the brim of the thread-
bare topper he took from beneath the bed whenever she paid a
visit. It made no difference. Danielle's mind was insurmountable.
Dull and hermetic—a little cocktail party. She could hardly conceive of him as being real.

Gilbert wondered why she inflamed him so. Thou doting fool,
forbear, forbear! Love is valid only in a pre-Revolutionary period.
Other old men he had known (or the men he'd thought of as old at
the time) would have been delighted with this gratuitous encore
on the part of the female species: a last look, devoid of lustful in-
tent, one more piece of luggage to hold dear in the memory while
moving on into dotage or death. So why then this concupiscence?
He couldn't believe it was his ridiculous body, his own biology,
that made him want to call her bluff, inflict his ancient ugliness on
Dani and probably rust in place on top of her. There was nothing
alive in him that wanted to fuck—or there wouldn't be, he rea-
soned, if he were a well man. Instead, when he should be enjoying
some quiescence, the fauna in his bloodstream, the spirochetes
and God knows what else, were squiggling over his brain, animat-
ing his lymph like a dybbuk making a man dance on broken legs.
They crowded into his crotch when Dani came in and fixed her bra
in front of his Louis XIV looking-glass (brought at great expense
from the Beltham estate, wrapped in down comforters and under
guard). *They* gave him nightmares of tumescence in his blackest
sleep, pharmaceutically induced, when nothing short of doomsday
should have been able to rouse him, and set him picking like a

young man through the few salacious memories he could still rec-
ollect, in the wet murk of his pillow, taking all the roles, like some
protean ogre—becoming So-and-so's enormous, almost muscular
breast, which she had rubbed against him like an ape, or perhaps
Pantry's twig-ish member, a live shoot from a dead tree, which
Gilbert had so often shrugged into a red handkerchief under a
tartan rug on the river . . . their punt drifting calamitously into
other boaters or knuckle-y root-matter, partially submerged, beneath the Spring-term sun.

It was *they*, those tiny creatures, who wanted out. They wanted
to outlive him. Louder than the rudest batch of sperm—though
with a contrary agenda—they pleaded to be sprayed into the
world: to consume innocent Danielle, eat their way right through
her, down to the last little hair that stuck like a signpost from
around the secret inner border under her skirt.

Gilbert's body was a machine for making disease. Lady Beltham
would have been proud. It was, in a sense, the purest, most animal form of revolt. Disease dissolves all the world's blockades—it
makes our innards into foreign territory. But Gilbert had for so
long considered *himself* a kind of infection, with these same cos-
mopolitan privileges, that his illnesses—which would certainly
kill him—felt something like a betrayal by his comrades.

Nevertheless, while they congregated in his carcass, showing
through the skin like red relief maps of the ocean floor, he could
still slip away from his troubles—the aches playing on his nerves,
those unwanted vistas of strap and contraption beneath Dani's
clothing—and sneak out through the ether to visit his many pro-
tégés, spy on and guide them, Gilbert the demiurge, far away as
a fish freezing solid on an Eskimo spear, near as an undergradu-

ate beaten green in the Latin Quarter. Under six down comforters and often too weak to hold a book, he was the nucleus of the
world-to-come.

Danielle was envied her special responsibility. She was never
bored with her mysterious charge. Unlike the other nurses, she
looked forward to coming to work in the morning, happy to hear
Gilbert talk, like the devotee of a television serial eager for her
next installment. It wasn't so much *what* he said, of course, but
how he spoke, which is to say gently, persuasively, distinguished
and dignified—despite the fact that beneath his quilt he was naked to the waist and thin as an insect wing. He spoke like they did
in the movies; he didn't ask or demand but insinuated, said things
like *We're probably just wicked enough to deserve each other Dani*, after
she'd told him of some indiscretion, a story she could never trust
to a peer.

Gilbert was a prize. There was no end to the backbiting that
went on in the clinic on the part of nameless girls who wanted to
take over Danielle's shift. They thought she did no work at all.
There were, however, her other patients: she had to think of them
too—couldn't just spend all day in Lord Whosis's room imbibing
of the atmosphere of catacombs. And Gilbert could be a handful:
he would put himself into raptures and need restraint, demanding
to phone his mother, whom he thought was a sprightly nonage-
narian hedonist living off her dividends in Biarritz, when she'd
been in the ground for more than a decade. He would "ring" for
Dani when she was on her break, or tending to someone else, or
off for the day, stamping his foot, as though she were his private
maid, infuriating his proud and Paris-trained inamorata. When
she chastised him he would pull handfuls of paper money from a
suitcase under his bed, its leather covered in the little bright land-

scapes of travel stickers from every continent and sea. She didn't really profit much by his generosity, as what he gave her was unusable: currency so exotic that the man at the bank had accused her of pulling a prank, assuring her there was no such country. If there had been, he'd have remembered. She was nearly arrested, and if it had gotten out that she'd taken money from a patient—even imaginary money—she would have been cashiered on the spot. It was best, therefore, not to encourage him, and easy enough to feign a certain disinterest—Dani had no stake in what he said, since it made no sense to her anyway. The most interesting thing about him was that he wanted so badly to be interesting.

Thinks he's God on high, she said to her colleagues, hoping to put them off the track. Breaks wind in the night and wakes up asking has the market crashed. Wets his bed and thinks it's the second deluge come. But try and keep him from the television or take his pens away, he looks at you like you've broke his heart. You should see it: he watches that TV like every newsflash is for him, like there wouldn't *be* any news if he stopped watching . . .

To desire reality is good! To realize one's desires is better. The police bore down on the marchers as they got back to the Sorbonne, where the gates were closed for the second time since the Plague (the first being when the Nazis took Paris). Barricades were erected, and the protestors settled in. The police attacked ambulances and reporters in their zeal, while the inhabitants of the Quarter opened their homes to the beleaguered students, giving them water and hiding them from the truncheon. Even Pantry's last lover, lost in the tumult, was rescued by a quiet family, his black armband misinterpreted as a token of solidarity, while just a few blocks distant the lover's wife was being run over by retreating rioters, panicked by rumors that the police would start using live ammunition. By the time the university was reopened, France had been paralyzed by a general strike. A medieval quiet came down on Paris: you could hear only human sounds, the gnashing of a few fires—on occasion the noise of middle-class automobiles fleeing for the country. The Sorbonne and environs became the headquarters of the movement, a citadel colored by student-made posters that would soon be ripped down and sold as collector's items.

The Théâtre de l'Odéon was occupied and became a place for debate and political song, open all day and night, hot and smelling like a full summer church. Jean-Louis Barrault, the Man in White, did not object: he took the stage and gave the theater away with his blessings, communicating through a prolonged mime that began with his separating himself, painlessly, like a baker would a wad of dough, first in two, then four, until the boards were mobbed with powdery Pierrots. Stepping on each other's tapered sandals, they wept calligraphically, then apologized to one another with great dignity and elegance, bowing low, lower, waiting with foreheads inches from the floor for another character to show up and topple them for a laugh. Since they were alone in their own company, however, they straightened up and leaned on each other, shoulder to shoulder, like the arches of a temple or a string of letter *M*s: pining, silent, a haunted facade.

Gilbert watched with admiration, inhabiting a cocky young philology student in the fifth row who was drying his palm by squeezing a ruined necktie in the pocket of his green cotton jacket, the sort of man his mother had still been marrying well into her sixties, doing her part during the Hitler War: self-assured, Mediterranean, and disoriented. The student didn't like the performance. It reminded him of the strange balletic movements in a silent film, and Youth, in its eternal present tense, found nothing relevant to its own experience in it—the little man had no time for antiquity. Gilbert wouldn't have wanted this otherwise. His children had to be free to play: to play with anything and everything without the hindrance of their parents' factitious respect for formulae with no applications.

(Still, taking his cue from the tyrants of the past—though he could never be a tyrant in a literal sense, his kingdom having no center or boundary—Gilbert allowed *himself* the privilege, verboten to his followers, of enjoying the grace, the quaintness, of obsolete forms. He had grown up in that world, after all, and its accent still affected him: the brittleness, the tremolo, the mayhem constrained in its imperfections. The hollow scratching of an Edison cylinder song coming up through the bloom of a black cone: this had been his earliest inspiration. He loved the nonsense signal pressing in on the orchestra as much as the tune they played, loved the dark inscrutability of dead-slow early filmstock as much as the peculiar faces the immature medium had singled out for adoration. In his new world, he would keep such treasures in a vault, in his hideaway, someplace tropical. He would bathe in their old light when the inscrutable sameness of his utopia became too much for his delicate dandy's temperament. And with his death, by and by, the last aesthete, the last apologist for nostalgia, the last commodity fetishist on Earth would be removed, leaving . . . something as yet unimaginable, even to him.)

He'd done some extras work in the pictures himself, Gilbert, on leave in Paris, away from the trenches. No footage remains, but I've found stills in the Cinémathèque Française that may substantiate this claim: a fuzziness with a homburg hat pulled down over its head-bandage, drinking schnapps in a frame dominated by the face of the great Musidora. This etude came after he'd been tossed out of Oxford, when he quit sucking dick and enlisted, in order to elude his mother, who swooped down wielding purse and title to set right the scandal he'd contrived, only to find that her son had sold most of his clothes and vanished.

Wadham, by the way, was the college to which the thirteen-year-old John Wilmot was admitted in 1660. Unlike Gilbert, who almost certainly considered Rochester to be one of his previous incarnations—the Earl's character too tasty, upon reflection, for the firm not to acquire—little John didn't get into serious trouble until after he'd been created a Master of Arts, when he and men both armed and masked abducted his future wife, then riding home fresh and full from dinner at Whitehall with her grandfather. Rochester took the heiress out of London in a black carriage with six horses and two ladies-in-waiting, shutting her, we imagine, in some lonely moor-side folly, hiding her from her other suitors and hoping to talk her into eloping. The Earl landed in the Tower of London for this within a week, too young to grow himself a prison beard, and Gilbert never took his degree.

Lady Beltham must have forgiven him—finding it necessary, I presume, to reward any act of her son's that compelled her to demolish a patrician prejudice—since Gilbert was put in charge of the bulk of the Beltham fortune as soon as he rang her solicitors in a panic from Verdun, desolate in a damp cranny north along the Meuse, on an improvised phone line, powered perhaps by blood sacrifice, strung along miles of intestine or nervous fiber, during a traitorous retreat with his regiment, having promised every man in his command he'd have them back in Paris by nightfall. He died a millionaire many times over, owning stock on every continent, and could, according to Danielle Renouard—who, shriveled, still lives in Berne—list every one of his holdings and their worth, like Charles Foster Kane, despite having no interest whatever in business, despite having no aptitude for sums or speculation.

He even had stock in Prosper Sforza's production company, though I wonder whether Danielle said this just to please me. She talked him into buying it herself, she claims, at the urging of her fiancé Ephraim, whose resume was so low in Sforza's stack of prospective art directors—having theretofore only worked on safety films and state television documentaries—he knew that he needed to bring something other than talent to the table. He hadn't heard of the Belthams, but had wormed from Dani the information that her favorite patient was titled and ate with his own silverware. She went to work on Gilbert, she wants me to tell you, as per her fiancé's instructions: lying about the prospects of the film's success, exaggerating its importance to her personally, and pretending not to feel the old man rub her bare knee with his wrist when she sat by his bed to watch him write the check. It arrived at Sforza's office in Rome clipped to another copy of Ephraim's resume. Prosper scribbled Gilbert an illegible receipt and told his secretary to write up a contract for Ephraim. How easy my job would be, he reflected, if all my applicants were as unmistakably gifted.

I told Renouard that her wealthy invalid might well have invested without her enticements, having so great an affinity with the film's protagonist; though it's true the same could have been said for Gilbert and virtually any figure of note. Our man's metaphysical holdings were just as vast as his stock portfolio, his theory of reincarnation—detailed at length in his memoirs—allowing him the widest possible selection of antecedents.

He figured that the process ran irrespective of our mortal perception of time: that the clockworks of it existed in a higher dimension, from which the whole of human history appeared as a static polygon, purple in color, each point of its volume a moment, each moment part of the mass of time, but existing in solid simultaneity, not burning up like successive lengths of fuse. This meant that it was just as likely that Herakleitos had had a soul originating in Erwin Schrödinger as vice versa, and, as such, that Gilbert could find in any person, living or dead, for whom he had some admiration, proof that the esteemed individual was an "earlier" incarnation of himself. Thus, the most brilliant achievements in the species' history—martial, technical, or aesthetic—could all be seen by Beltham as triumphs in his own quite personal saga, and pleasure taken in them, as the memory of having once baked a particularly good soufflé at home might enhance your enjoyment of a professional's.

Beltham was certain, for instance, that his biological father had been a version of his own well-seasoned soul, at a point perhaps three-quarters of the way through its evolution. He'd never met the man, but his mother had told him stories that put to pale the pabulum his schoolmates bought and reread in the dormitory until the taupe paper of their magazines had turned transparent from contact with kiddy oil. While they devoured the expensive exploits of the occult detective Doctor Silence, or the hideous, unimaginably cruel Don Quebranta Huesos, Beltham spent pennies at the newsagent's, investing in the phlegmatic daily news to read with grim satisfaction as one patsy after another was executed in his father's place. *Crime is the highest form of sensuality.*

Gilbert often wondered whether the reason that certain people welcomed his influence, while others were immune, was that his followers were in fact ancient, infantile incarnations of himself— some of the first out of the shop. If this was true, then Gilbert was an army all to himself: not a man but a multitude, an unsanitary aggregate, united in strife, inventing a clumsy new language for the world.

But this hypothesis raised a new question. If a soul could be stretched so very thin—made to serve over and over again, in the same eras, like a string looped tightly through the strata on a pegboard, crossing its own path to make a design—was he unique in having lived so many lives, or was the tally of souls at large so tiny as to make this program necessary? Perhaps there was a shortage. How many, then, were out there? A thousand spread through history? A hundred? Less? Or could it be the world was split neatly in two? Divided between Gilbert the radical and some stodgy, inertial nemesis, forever running his progress to ground?

And then, what if there was only one? The question was inevitable. One soul in the world, doing endless duty, from subterranean Lascaux to suburban Los Angeles, from Sappho to Chuck Berry. What if all the known Gilberts were merely the tiny, conscious tip of a vast and sunken agglutination of Gilberts-past? What if it was he himself, incarnated as a misguided bureaucrat— in a life so deeply buried, so early in his private history that he was unable to infiltrate it or bring it to light—who was denying *this* Gilbert, *our* Gilbert, permission to return to France? Or he who—as Danielle—gave him his injections and pills and peeks, always bending and stretching and giddily lascivious, yes, because luxuriating, just out of the cosmic womb, in his newfound corporeality, like an infant tangled in its sheets, palpating the palms of its hands?

It would mean that the world was created old. That he was the agent of exhaustion, not renewal. He should have welcomed this concept as the culmination of his personal philosophy—no center

and no boundary—but the traffic of his thought skirted this re-
ductio ad absurdum as it would the terrain of an old humiliation.
When it found itself straying too near, or facing it outright, he
would hiss and cuss in the foulest words of five languages to divert its attention: twitching his head, upsetting his topper, scaring
Dani into calling the doctor and the doctor into recommending
a different anti-inflammatory. Over time his ration of sedatives
was steadily increased until Dani worried his charm would be
squeezed out completely. But Gilbert didn't mind. He did his best
work in a proper stupor. Tranquil, he'd tap with two fingers one of
the less likely cities on his suitcase. Have you been? he would ask
her. No? We two must go someday.

6
Wilhelmina Princep

Her first husband was hanged. She got her title from him, and much of her fortune, to which was added in time a small annuity on account of his wrongful arrest. After he'd "danced the Paddington frisk," she traveled to the Normandy coast and married the father of her son at a secret ceremony in front of the local curé and two witnesses they recruited from a farmer's bar. Their priest volunteered in good cheer to be murdered as soon as the toast was drunk, being famous in those parts as a gossip and unwilling to swear in good faith not to brag about what he'd been party to. As it would mean bad luck to kill again, the witnesses lost only their ring fingers, which they saw wrapped in blue ribbon and put in the honeymoon luggage along with the writ they'd signed before the chop. Properly marinated and spun on hatpins, the fingers could be used as compasses that would point them out wherever they hid, and they endured a short lecture on the proper way to prepare these as well as the punishments in store if they broke their oaths and blabbed . . . bleeding all the while into bridal-garter tourniquets, which Wilhelmina graciously allowed them to keep as souvenirs. They all combed the grass and sand with rakes to erase any signs of their assembly, and buried the curé in a sitting position with the leftover wine. It was a June wedding.

On their way south the newlyweds pierced the ears of a childless couple in Quimper, and with a hand drill ran a long, sharp filigree chain through a broad iron weight, a bedpost, and then one of the feet of Gilbert's crib—shipped specially from England—making a taut scalene triangle with the captives strung on its longest line. The babysitters were left two tall milking stools for sleeping and only enough play in the chain to let them fetch food to the crib, if they moved in concert, and water from the pump. Bride and groom left for Egypt, following by design the route taken by the author of *Salammbô* while he was researching his book and contracting syphilis. The groom's resolution that they avoid expensive European accommodations and stay only in brothels or rooming houses on their honeymoon was motivated by malice and expediency in equal measure (she had to learn about doing without, and harlots were cheaper than hotels), but ensured too that they must at some point have shared a bed with Gustave's ghost. Whether it was he or the Egyptian fleas that needled at her through the night, Wilhelmina itched so terribly that she finally climbed through the window to camp out on the iron trellis—shaped like a conch—bolted to the face of the building. In nightgown, top sheet, and mosquito netting, hair loose and levitating in the heat, she hung suspended over the empty souk, enormously uncomfortable, braced only at the small of her back: a flyblown Pre-Raphaelite sprite. Three native amateur photographers captured her thus from their bedroom windows, darkening their ceiling paper with ash from their flash powder and causing Wilhelmina to dream of heat lightening over her ancestral home in Berne—a fact she confided to her infant son in a letter he could not have hoped to read, which I have here, along with the photos, pinned to a corkboard over my bed. (They ought to be in plastic.)

All the pimps, madams, and bawds knew the groom by sight, while the station agents knew Wilhelmina, the Belthams and Princeps having advertised for her safe return through the colonial offices of all the great European powers—since her "rape," if legitimized, would place the Beltham fortune gallingly outside their reach. Rather than abandon his plan to travel by rail (negotiating North Africa by coach would be tiresome and sweltering, not to mention expensive, and moreover would have been quite in Wilhelmina's mode, as she was a great lover of carriages and a past master of their etiquette: the smile or nod to admirers at crosswalks, the hand extended with alms or billet-doux), the bridegroom dressed her in muslin slacks and a chauffeur's cap and took to calling her Bill. He explained to their hoteliers that she was his dissolute English brother and that he'd been charged by their father with keeping her on the straight and narrow during their stay: a task that was proving so difficult (she'd sneak out the window, he said, down drainpipes and even slatted tile, had drugged his milk and left him snoring on a bench by the consulate after they'd picked up their month's allowance) that he'd given it up entirely, and indeed under duress had taken on the role of her procurer, the better to protect her from wog thugs and thieves.

She didn't mind the name—her sisters had called her Bill—but the idea was ridiculous: who could mistake her for a man? That sort of thing only worked on stage. But the more she tried to exaggerate her femininity, the more her husband's story was taken for true; if there was any doubt in their audience's mind about this smooth and alluring youth—whose face in particular, avian and to-the-point, advertised her proper sex—her performance removed it. In a borrowed waistcoat, her repertoire of coquettish smirks and silly demurrals, perfected during her years as a demi-mondaine, put all comers in mind of a first-rate fop, prompting the stationmasters to blush and the bawds to offer winsome Bill a free first turn with any girl in the house.

Forced thus to contend with the slaver of Arab whores—who made her their pet and cosseted her shamelessly, locking her in their boudoirs, insisting that she teach them what her London ladies did, pinning, kissing, and tickling her like the Princep cousins had in their old attic—as well as the bridegroom's evident familiarity with such houses: his easy humor with their proprietors, who hadn't been beautiful since before Napoleon I, calling them not just by name but by juvenile diminutives they blushed to be reminded of—Bill was a little put out. And these weren't her only complaints. She was beginning, as familiarity cleared her sight, to observe a number of unsettling similarities between her new beau and dead Beltham. While there was every evidence that one was the devil himself and the other had just been an agreeably baffled Privy Councilor, both—far from showing the horror of Dean Swift's Strephon at knowing that "Celia, Celia, Celia shits!"—took a rather off-putting interest in *all* the stations of her toilette. Both paid her hindquarters a dedicated attention, bordering on the medical (if no less lubricious for this precision), studying her over the chamber pot so intently she could only thank the Lord that she'd grown up with so many sisters and was consequently inured to the experience, even a little pleased to have the luxury of finding this behavior more puzzling than humiliating.

Rather more vexing, however, was the fact that they would only give equal consideration to those impedimenta unique to a Wilhelmina once a month, insisting on having their way with her while she was "having the painters in"—as her father Sir Pritchard Princep (or "Pilchard," as he was known in the family, on account of his fishy dithering and bullet-shaped head) would have put it—a concession which had taken some getting used to and that she still found rather dubious. In the end she suspected that neither did these arsyversy things out of an innate disposition toward conflating the erotic with the excretory—or merely messy—but because, for the bridegroom, it was "revolutionary" ("infinitely more pessimistic, and therefore more poetic," and in the latter instance explicitly forbidden by Mosaic law), and, for the departed, merely "naughty," and this realization was a blow.

After circumstances forced her to fuck a pretty Moroccan conversant in six languages with the curl of a belt on loan from her husband, she fled to Cairo with their money and papers—a Mrs. Erhebung of the Quai de Commerce, Brussels, wife of a catalog indexer and mother of one—fully expecting that she'd be pursued with fluency and that this reunion would present an opportunity for renegotiating the terms of their relationship. Seven days of luxuriating in solitude on indoor plumbing at the Grand Concorde left her destitute and demoralized; she went to the consulate to wire her solicitor for ready money, but her assets had been frozen pending the resolution of her "abduction." To the Princeps she sent lies and affirmations of chastity bolstered by intermittent and irate indictments of their lack of trust, hoping to persuade them to forward money but leave her at liberty long enough to be retrieved by her hubby. Waiting for her family's next riposte she met the first of five further husbands drinking mint tea on a bench outside the consulate: a Cambridge-educated Egyptian stockbroker and poet who took note of her despond and pitied her. His courtship was swift and determined. Anticipating a future caught in Araby, a life of blistering feet and itinerant litigation, fighting the Princeps for cash while crisscrossing the desert ahead of a choking wind of over-polite creditors, each bearing hotel bills in green ink on cream paper, twisted cleverly around sticky walnut, honey, and cardamom candies, and finally a descent to the level of her spotty bedmates in those bawdy houses—each of whom, she could well believe, had been royalty before embarking on some ill-considered elopement—she saw little advantage in protesting that she was taken.

This one's particular hobby was the collection and restoration of antique medical paraphernalia, which delighted Wilhelmina with its specificity. The night of their wedding he presented her with a priceless bronze seventeenth-century codpiece designed to prevent masturbation, which he then strapped on and went through inordinate pains to make love to her with and through. On a marble shelf were ivory figurines the length of her palm— pretty brittle maids covering their breasts or pressing modest mouths—but whose diffidence came off with the lids of their bellies, disclosing a fingernail fetus swimming over hand-painted bowels (baby and bowels likewise detachable for closer scrutiny).

The new honeymoon brought Wilhelmina back to England, where her Egyptian collapsed in their parlor while trying to fit himself into a silver mask he'd acquired from an antiques dealer who'd dropped by especially to sell it. It was a prototype training helmet built with subscription money—in the very literal sense that the currency was melted and poured into molds—by a Scots clergyman in 1808, designed to keep a young girl's mouth immobile and discourage her from raising her head. The Egyptian's favorite doctor was summoned from his private clinic on the island of Samos, in sight of Turkey and only a ten-minute walk from the temple of Hera. He wired instructions that the patient not be moved and arrived four days later with a blacksmith in tow to remove the apparatus with tongs and pliers. Finally he knelt down on the Oriental rug to diagnose a series of strokes. Asked if he was suffering, the dying man replied that it was about as bad as an insignificant pain could be—on a par with a sore or boil, but deep behind his forehead, which had been checkered with rows of maroon and tarnish-green bruises by the restraints. After the Egyptian's eyes had been closed, the doctor consoled Wilhelmina by pointing out that if the pain had been great for a superficial complaint, it followed that it must have been rather trivial for a mortal one, and consequently that his passing had been mild.

Gilbert was rescued and deposited with one of his aunts. Single for a year then and in full possession of her fortune, Wilhelmina moved to Paris to provoke her family and start a salon. When the smitten Samos sophist came after her, she proposed to him as an inventive *blague* for the benefit of her new friends and found in him by chance a most sympathetic mate. While her arriving guests were escorted out of her lift and shown to their seats by her footmen, she parted green and lilac curtains thicker than asbestos, showing one coy eye and a solid unfashionable polygon of straight blonde hair to the Boulevard Malesherbes, on the lookout for her real husband, whom she saw sharpening knives in every shadow, while the doctor—the dear—unused to servants, served orangeade, petit fours, and strychnine with lemon (a tonic for dip-

somaniacs), lighting cigars as necessary and seeming as charming
to the Parisians, in his way, as the reproduction of a sculpture
unearthed on his island that sat in the foyer.

He was a pleasure—better than entertaining, he thought up
ways for her to entertain herself. He appreciated Wilhelmina's
particular wit and encouraged her to write a roman à clef about
her time in the Orient. She wrote it in French, which he couldn't
read, as the "Duchesse de Maquette," taking much license with the
facts. After the sudden death of her prospective publisher she put
the book aside for fifty years, bringing it out at her own expense
in an edition of two thousand, of which five hundred were printed
on green paper, signed in a hand like a seismograph needle, and
sent to friends and relatives, most of whom were ignorant of the
true identity of the mysterious Duchesse and so destroyed or returned the slim little book on receipt. (Mine is the 1985 Virago
Press reprint.)

The doctor was round and bald and gold and full of trivia,
which he pronounced in a buzzing, uncertain English that seemed
to come from his trunk instead of his throat, like the chirp of a
mechanical bird. He drew her attention one night to the fact that
the sludge of a nighttime sneeze on his nightshirt was indistinguishable to the eye, after a few days, from that of his semen, and
she was quick to put this memento mori into her novel, in the
mouth of her abductor, whom she'd cast not as an inscrutable ci-
pher but a munificent maniac and boor. Full of rhetoric, her hero
was as preoccupied with justifying his gargantuan appetites as he
was with satisfying them—and, for preference, doing both at once:
lecturing on Ruskin and the morality of form while violating from
behind a schoolgirl bound hand and foot with thorny creepers, a

goblet in one hand and a clarinet in the other. His wife, made to watch and listen, kept her sanity by planning escape.

They summered in Baden-Salsa. With Wilhelmina in bed with migraine, the doctor on a midday walk took a path that went bad. He was found fully dressed but pale as linden, having been slavered every inch with a lady's lead-based face cream: waylaid, stripped, and—shivering in the sun—made to pull his suit on again at pistol-point. Her next husband was the investigating sergeant. He proposed during the inquest and made Wilhelmina feel safe. His mother had been a Russian governess in Berlin, herself looking after the children of an English governess who had eloped with her employer. The daughter of muzhiks, pinched and resolute, she had taught him French and German with picture books of the Golden Horde. After being wounded in the knee during a raid on a bathhouse he had been retired to the undemanding and much-envied position of chief detective of the resort constabulary. He was nearer her age than any of the preceding husbands but so proper and old fashioned that he might as well have been her father. He refused to come visit her in Paris and sent her staccato love notes via telegraph. They married the following year in the hotel chapel, and though his skin was thick and muddy, a small poisonous thorn wormed through the back of his hand during a honeymoon picnic and left him raving. He became convinced that Wilhelmina was made of clay: she had to be submerged and smoothed down and then eaten while soft and cool in order to fill his stomach for the long ride back to Berlin. He forced his new wife to the artificial lake and was restrained by three bellboys midway through the process of drowning her. In custody he refused to let them pull out the thorn and died with it still stuck in, thirty years later, occupying a room very near Wilhelmina's only son, with the incident classified by his successor at the station as misadventure due to heat stroke.

The Great War came and men became scarce, relieving Wilhelmina of the responsibility of swearing off them for their own good. She moved home and volunteered, very fetching in a paper Red Cross bonnet, her mornings spent with soldiers complaining of the cacophony of early spring birdsong as the sky warmed up at ten-to-five: their eardrums punctured by the bass of Big Bertha—anyway having adapted to the lower frequencies of battlefields—they found the piping chilly and shrill, even painful, and asked Wilhelmina to organize the sisters into scarecrow details, regularly firing the officers' service revolvers into the air at first light, making tunnels of sun in the haze and causing approaching ambulances to circle the hospital in terror.

Their fevers and insomnia making 3 A.M. to dawn the optimal time for sleep, the wounded bristled too at the earlier dawn come spring, and asked Wilhelmina to institute a local "darkness-savings time"—to keep the hospital an hour ahead of the surrounding townships, with the soldiers' bones thus an hour closer to knitting—and to paint the windows black. Lyric Nurse Princep on aching feet watched the mist rising off the plains as she inked away the countryside with an old roof-tar brush and tried to remember whether the earth being warmer than the air or vice versa caused this phenomenon. She didn't marry an ailing soldier but woke up lonesome in the '20s and so left the family seat to re-enter society. Taking her handsome son's advice to marry only men she wanted to see buried, she enjoyed twenty years of luxurious widowhood before seizing on the perfect subject for experimentation during the London Blitz. An arms dealer and black marketeer, he was a sturdy Italian boy tanned almost to maroon, with a taste for gaudy clothing and bad English, affecting the accent of a Cockney ponce and dressing in such fluorescence that many a block warden forbade him to walk their districts for fear of attracting fire. (Where did he get his tan? There wasn't any sun. Where did he get his clothing? None was being made.) He sold tainted aspirin, rancid cooking oils, and coffee crawling with worms; they met during a performance of *Orphée et Eurydice* that was bombed out, with only the singers, stagehands, Wilhelmina, and her future husband keeping their seats during the attack (he because he was courting a chorus girl, she because she'd rather have died than let Gluck be performed to an empty house). Masonry fell around them and shrapnel hobbled three satyrs. When a V-2 fell close enough that a burnt page from the user's manual was later found plastered over the marquee, Wilhelmina and the Italian were startled into noticing one another.

He was half her age and common as the cold. They bought a stalker's cabin in darkest Scotland to get away from the war and passed a year hunting hare, with the Italian trying diligently to father a race of titled daughters on his aging wife and Wilhelmina meanwhile waiting for him to expire in some nicely exotic way. By the time the Americans entered the war, she'd run out of patience. She paid him off and sent him packing, wiring Gilbert—who was away founding a totalitarian utopia in southern Chile—that he owed her for her wasted time.

There were many lovers, and she continued to attract them, but only married once more. This last was younger than her son: a Flemish Jew, working for the state film board, whom she caught trying to filch a Daumier bust when his television crew came to photograph the treasures of the Princep house for a documentary.

(I recommend the tour, which is free on Thursdays.) He wanted to paint, and she was pleased to pay his way, but he wouldn't drop his steady girlfriend, who took to lurking around the estate in various guises—a maid and then a serving girl, a chauffeur or sous chef—until Wilhelmina finally ordered them both off the premises, her staff linking hands and making a chain, flushing them out the front gate.

Her letters would fill several volumes. Most were to her son. The last is halting and strange. (I'm immune to peeping at the last page of novels ahead of time, but can't help turning to the end of letter collections first thing, curious to see whether my celebrity had any inkling that this RSVP would be his last, eager to take in the irony of a rendezvous cheerily promised or else the prescience of a pessimistic farewell.) Prompted by something she doesn't record—a sound, probably, in her empty house—she wonders to Gilbert whether the exiled couple could have snuck back, and with foul play in mind. She jokes that she could end up like the narrators of those horror stories who take the time to record their suspicions rather than act on them: sitting and writing when the sensible thing would be to lock the door, call for help, or just get up and run. How you'd laugh, she writes, if this letter ended in the phonetic transcription of my death agony. But then: There it is again. I'll ring for the servants.

Wilhelmina stopped writing and walked into the corridor—a tube, padded and purple, like the sleeve of her dressing gown. She called, but her voice didn't carry. She went back to her desk and wrote: I'm certain that someone's in here with me. Then: I'm afraid it isn't whom I expected. I'll come back and finish this later.

7
Ephraim Bueno

When in a novel or anecdote your narrator tells you he's stopped, on his way out of the house, in the kitchen, to make sandwiches, the kitchen you agree is a plausible setting probably has no hollowware in its cabinets or unscoured pots on the range: it's entire and ideal, a perfection in your head that would only be soiled by details. Green tile, faux-marble cutting boards, insect-encrusted light fixtures and so forth would demand all the rest: four walls, a ceiling, doors and windows, dishes in the sink, and the smell of take-out slinking from the garbage bin. Still, we don't complain: it isn't necessary that we see this kitchen clearly. As a model, it functions. It is evocative. Put too much pressure on it, though—this mode of perceiving imaginary space—and it starts to get uncomfortable. We squirm. It feels a little like fitting broken lead back into the beak of a mechanical pencil.

For instance. Imagine please a kitchen countertop with implements haphazardly placed. (Maybe the drawers are getting aired or papered. Maybe someone's about to cook an elaborate dinner.)

Sounds easy, but for me it's like Borges and his flock of birds. He sees a flock fly by (when he could still see). There can't have been more than ten of them, but trying to remember later exactly how many there were, he finds that every integer in the set {1–10} looks indisputably wrong. There weren't one or two or three or nine, and yet there were certainly—he's positive!—less then ten. He's only comfortable leaving the question alone: settling for a blurry, indeterminate digit like a partial erasure—an impression of quantity just specific enough to resist estimation. In the end, all he's really certain of is what numbers it wasn't.

My counter is gray. On it, without effort, I see a bouquet of white cylindrical grips: gears and triggers as on ice-cream scoops, wire as on cheese-slicers, cupolas as on juicers, bulbs as on basters, cranks as on grinders, tapered holes as on graters, but *not* slicers, scoops, basters, grinders. The familiar elements don't adorn anything familiar; the objects are indefinite, murky, impossible. Pick one up or peer at it too closely and it falls apart like a moth's wing. Imagined as a whole, "a countertop with kitchen implements," my mind puts together a kind of theatrical contrivance: good enough from a distance, but not to be scrutinized . . . a number that's less than ten, but also isn't any of the numbers between ten and zero. Good. But what if someone insists?

Pity Ephraim Bueno, then, who found himself in charge of designing the entire film, sets through costumes, and was appointed property manager to boot. By "designing," Sforza meant collecting, foraging: there wasn't a construction budget, wasn't a painting budget or petty cash for purchases; every cent Bueno spent would come out of some other budget, so the crew spied on him, sent relatives to threaten his carpenters, tore up his drawings of Rochester's wallpaper or King Charles's riding cloak. He'd wanted to paint, wanted to fake the famous portraits the movie would need to hang on manor walls, to make the royal crest and do trompe l'oeil on joists and moldings in the cheap, ugly rooms Sforza had rented, to cheat them into the eighteenth century. Instead he had to read the script and find in every casual description—a countertop, a doctor's bag, a gun cabinet, or a stable—cause for a kind of vertigo, as though he was leaning into a ravine. Where Myrna the writer saw space filled—wasn't it enough to *get* the characters into a kitchen? to know what they *did* there?—Ephraim saw only emptiness, protoplasm, the dawn of the world, swimming with slippery, unrealized chimera.

Worse, it was a *period* film—another layer of abstraction. He couldn't get just any potato peeler: it had to be a Restoration potato peeler. He complained to Dani and she reminded him he was there to do a job: why should it be easy? She thought she'd earned herself a special dispensation, having laundered so many crazy men's shat drawers and fed them by hand at the risk of her fingers. She'd acquired like a smoker's clothes the smell of the asylum, mildewed but antiseptic—impossible to wash out. Rescued now, she didn't want to do anything but eat and sleep and putter around the apartment, keep it homelike despite the debris—didn't even want to fuck. She leaned reading on her naked elbows out their second story window upwards of twelve hours a day, listening after dark to night birds or tree frogs or adenoidal stranglers chirping in the Bois de Vincennes.

With Foche, Ephraim drank grappa and grumbled, just across the street. Sforza sent out memos on mosquito-bite-pink carbon paper that the film was alive and well but would take a while to find its feet after the riots. He promised retainers and per diems and asked that everyone stay put: trying, or so Foche theorized, to alienate the big down-on-his-luck English actor Wexler had hired cheap from out a sex scandal, trying to get his girlfriend Evelyn and other naughty baggage from his Italian projects into the film now that the strikes had given him an opening, now that their original leading lady was in a cast. Was he having second thoughts? Why not just relocate to Italy, asked some, where Sforza had friends on backlots, had stages and a studio? The question made Prosper fidget. He'd talked Foche into buying him a pistol. The cast and crewmembers with better prospects found new work and left town as soon as the trains were running. Those who remained were either Parisians with other means of support, or those, like Ephraim, with nowhere else to go.

The café's patronne, a Chilean witch, called Dani *putain* for having her morning coffee half dressed and at midday and half out that window, plain to see in the summer light and from a bag of instant. Leprous, she said—look at her skin. I could pinch it right off. No wonder she wants sun. And that rickety sill—she'll fall into the street. The ambulance men wait years for such delights . . . you don't know what they do while you're dozing. Polite Foche spat on her floor to distract her, said to Bueno, hey, look, she doesn't know it's your lady.

Tipsy at 10 A.M., soaking cigarettes in their spills on the Formica when the patronne took away their ashtray, they joked to each other that their problems were theology. Your director says, "Let there be light!"—all right, fine, but what kind, what color, and who goes to fetch it? Do you make it yourself, or buy it off the rack—and who pays? Then birds, beasts, the trees and their fruit, the waters and Leviathan whose tail wraps around the world: these are serious expenses. This production is getting out of hand.

They never drank anything that wasn't from a bottle: they knew the patronne whitened her café au lait with powdered egg when the milkman wanted paying. She pretended to dislike them, Foche and Bueno, but they were handy and diverting and anyhow wholly resistant to neglect and invective. She could refuse to serve them, throw a plate at them, even kick their table over, and still they'd sit on, sipping, playing checkers, chuckling at their jokes and poking each other's shoulders. After hours of her sulks and demands and threats they'd excuse themselves, beatific, when a runner came from Sforza, or Foche's wife Eugenia sent their fat son, or because they just felt like stretching their legs: paying the check, pushing their chairs back in place, and leaving the café so gingerly that the bells on her door didn't ring.

Short on money during those months of waiting, Ephraim helped the patronne manage her neighborhood feuds, so numerous that the logistics would have overwhelmed her if she'd had to keep the books herself. He made her misanthropy fantastically efficient, leaving notes as to who'd slighted her or who he'd heard her threaten, buying a notebook to use as a ledger and updating it once a week, adding names when she'd sworn some new revenge and removing them when a hecatomb was offered to appease her. She was feared in the neighborhood now that she had this auxiliary memory, and treated, if not with respect, than with a certain delicacy.

Foche told tall tales, most culled from his two years of national service, when as a stocky transplanted Parisian with a yen to study mathematics he'd been sent back to the land of his birth to shoot at nationalists. These were average stuff, about narrow streets that vanished after a single visit, women he'd slept with who proved to be ghosts (young Raoul always finding their parents or obituaries or crumbling portraits by chance, walking back to the barracks after waking up alone and standing sadly naked on his hotel balcony, calling out whatserface's name), strong drinks insurrectionists had sold to Europeans laced with dormant insect eggs, treasure maps calculated to unravel men's minds with their inexhaustible convolutions, sea monsters, wells leading to underground cities sculpted from rock salt and discarded rolling paper, mile-long giants sleeping under the sands of the desert—discovered when his regiment blundered into a yawning nostril—and outposts emptied to a man overnight by winds lifting the soldiers like eagles out to crack a tortoise.

But Foche was ambidextrous; neither his hands nor his brain knew right from left, and as a kid he'd inverted the order of letters and sentences to such a degree that he was functionally illiterate into his teens, reading and writing an almost-accurate patois based on shape and pattern recognition—living only on the surface of words, their similarities as pictograms, eventually as sounds, rather than their corresponding, representational content. This peculiarity extended beyond literacy: having learned to organize his thoughts according to broad categories and correspondences—the shapes of ideas, filed according to his own idiosyncratic method of cataloging—Raoul would interrupt a story involving—say—a stray dog with a broken and dragging leg, seen drinking from a sewer in Oran at dawn, to begin six other stories concerning dogs or legs, fusty water, curbs, cities, the qualities of morning sunlight in North Africa, the tune he'd whistled as he walked, and so forth. If a listener interrupted to ask for the point or punchline of the initial yarn, Raoul lost his train of thought entirely, looking as confused and affronted as someone sidetracked by a rude non sequitur.

While he yarned, Yevgennie was always at large, following the clicks of his claws across the arcs of warped hardwood that usefully directed all spills out the door and into the gutter. Both courteous and demanding, like displaced royalty, he shoved his tiny trapezoidal head into any dangling hand, instigating a petting or else marking every customer with the glands in his cheeks, appointing a court in exile. The patronne kept a broom handy to brain the little prince if he came too near, and like an adolescent boy strained forward on the front legs of her barstool to savor every dirty word or blue anecdote Foche might touch on in his narrative perambulations.

July simmered on, the city hesitant as its reflection in the skin of an oil slick and likewise smelling of melted rubber and peony. The 13th arrondissement fell under the shadow of the Bric-a-Brac Bandit, while Foche for his part was inspired to make a survey of every American detective story that employed the conceit of a culprit's using Independence Day fireworks to mask the sound of gunfire. Ephraim and Dani's rooms began to resemble a sweltering life-size Cornell box, filling with items filched from homes left unlocked as the Parisians sweated on their terraces or front steps, drinking beer and wondering at the motives of this genteel thief who stole only silverware, picture frames, old buttons, bottles—more like a ragman than a burglar. It fostered over time the belief that some lucky household might be harboring a treasure, tarnished to an inauspicious color or forgotten in the back of a drawer, wrapped in canvas and worth a king's ransom: the real target of the Bandit's baffling bad taste. Nothing else made sense.

On more than one occasion, when the heat should have made it think twice, the neighborhood tore at itself, like a dog trying to

remove its own collar, ransacking its attics and cellars and hidey-
holes for the least hint of this mythical fortune-in-a-teaspoon—
tortured by the thought that one of them might be sitting on a
million unawares. These impromptu, drunken treasure hunts
made Ephraim's scavenging even easier, since most of the ancient junk the local families excavated got left stacked in heaps on
the street corners for collection, caricaturing in their brown and
dusty disrepair the buildings from which they'd been exhumed.
The soil and smell of the early twentieth century was expelled
into the summer air and like scrim hung there to give Bueno some
shade as he tiptoed around and took his pick. At home Danielle
arranged his spoils absently against the walls and rehearsed in the
mirror what she'd say when the police finally came round. She
thought crime was Ephraim's way of sublimating his frustration
with her; later she characterized her continuing carnal disinterest
to me as a desire to see how far she could push him. But there was
no pleasure for Bueno in his success as a sneak thief. He was shor-
ing up against the demands of Wexler and Sforza: laying in a store
of the miscellaneous for winter.

   After he hit her drunk one evening with the base of a brass
lamp that she hadn't found room for, ripping its variegated paper
shade and twisting its tasseled pull strings into a knot, Danielle
wondered too whether there might be a genetic component to
Ephraim's magpie behavior. Had some twenty-score-great-grand-
father done the same? The surname would indicate he'd let himself be baptized to avoid expulsion from Spain under Ferdinand, in
the *annus mirabilis* 1492. She could see him as a rich Marrano—a
convert who'd kept his old religion in secret. Had he taken trades
from like-minded neighbors for ready cash as the Inquisition bore
down? Perversely increasing his load when he needed most to be

unencumbered? She imagined this ur-Bueno's own belongings waiting to be packed into trunks, mingling everywhere with those incursions from other houses, suggesting a man with twenty lives and families limp behind him like peacock feathers. Then the sullen ur-Bueno and estate on a rasping galleon, bound north by water from Cadiz, around the fingers of Europe, almost sinking the ship with his hoard. Lighting a taper to read by, he finds the nighttime deck so dim that his lamp and those of the sailors on watch seem to share one light between them, the waxing of one in the Atlantic breeze making the others dim and go out. Dani saw the legacy of this gray-maned charcoal sketch she'd invented stand out clearly in the gangly mantis she was all but married to. There would be no changing him.

They'd been with each other five years. He'd always been as aimless and opportunistic—often quoting P. A. Renoir's dictum that a man live his life like a river-borne cork, content to be pushed by the current. Whistling with pain—the Buenos having a predisposition to rotten teeth—he'd gone to see a dentist only when his then-girlfriend at the Kunstgewerbeschule Zurich had forced him to, promising to pick up the check. Danielle was working in the office as a receptionist and nurse; her main duties were to steam Herr Doktor's instruments and help him on with his tie in the mornings, the poor man praying all the while that she wouldn't notice the erection mussing the crease of his worsted trousers and nipping at her hipbones, those tiny handlebars in her frock. They were flagrante in this position when the classmates came in, Ephraim leaning on his shorter, slighter, stouter girl and biting his lip as though already embarrassed at the scene he'd shortly witness.

Witnessing it, squeaking down on the orange plastic sofa in

the waiting room, he poked his lady draughtsman sugar-momma
in the shoulder, calling her attention to the egg-shaped dentist
with tiny beak swelling his shell at groin-level—Dani towering
over him, rebuttoning his collar and looking likely to put a kiss
on his pate when she finished. As the two left the bathroom, Dani
first, backlit by her employer's blush, Ephraim wondered aloud
how many years it had been since there was sawdust on the surgery floor to soak up blood and spit. The dentist's tools could be
spied on their tray through the open surgery door, freshly sterile
hors d'oeuvres at hand by the adjustable chair—menacing in its
subdued and marshy leather-tones by contrast to the comic book
primaries of the waiting room. With Eph strapped in, looking
with his art student's eye at the blades and pliers on offer at a
gentle angle, wondering would he be able to sketch them from
memory if asked, Dani tied a white paper bib around his throat
and on impulse moistened her clean index finger and wrote her
name invisibly in the grease on his forehead. A mistake. He followed her home.

But when his next infatuation came along, and all the others after—cork-Ephraim looking to wash further downstream—Dani
found she couldn't let him go. It wasn't hard to keep him: all she
had to do was distract him, divert his attention, make enough of a
show of herself that the path of least resistance would lead without
doubt back to Danielle. (Often it was enough just to repaint the
kitchen.) Even Wilhelmina, the old rich woman, wasn't enough of
an eddy to separate them, though it was a pretty close call—with
will-less Eph swearing and swearing to each in turn that he'd
never see the other again, his preferences so provisional that he
didn't doubt his own sincerity, even after he'd shown Dani his
wedding ring, after he'd moved into that mammoth house—even

that first time he'd come home from rapacious Wilhelmina, just a set-dresser then on starvation wages: so pleased to have been asked back to the mansion for a quiet dinner, begging Dani's permission in all innocence to go back alone to spend time with the old woman—and really, what could be the harm in that? Dani was even invited to the wedding.

Having quit that first real job on the documentary crew to become lord of Wilhelmina's manor—after his arts degree had bought him years of dishwashing and retail and We Regret We Must rejections by post—he snuck Dani in the servants' entrance at the first opportunity. She left her dentist reluctantly, but enjoyed the game of her new life: she and Eph fucked in the kitchen and the attic (big as a hangar, and a museum of two centuries' worth of passé or objectionable art and furniture, divans aplenty, and Dani's ass coming away clotted with paisley dust from under a bust of *Der Führer*), the maid's quarters and the garage (in the back of the old woman's Hispano-Suiza, frictionless with mink oil), in, under, and out of every imaginable service uniform, frilly or starched. And, best of all, she had time to herself now, to read and to think in her own little room, wooden and resonant, half-underground, which the other servants complained of as being too crypt-like, but was a delicious hidey-hole to have during those hours Ephraim was engaged with his lady wife. Eph and Dani were devastated when they were finally caught and thrown out. Even their clothes were estate property.

Dani holding a nursing license, she took the first position she could find: a job with the Sanatorium, still not much more than a maid. Unlikely she'd last more than six months, said the supervisor, likely too she'd lose at least a fingertip. Where was Eph? At home, brooding and lonely: painting pornographic tailor's dummies and abandoning them on street corners as guerrilla art. Three years later, in Paris, when Foche's wife Eugenia arrived after Ephraim had hit Dani to console the girl and dress her wound—the gory lamp lying shattered in the bathtub—Dani revised her diagnosis a third time. Not sexual frustration and not heredity: Eph must be having an affair with Eugenia. How else could she have known to come so quickly? Dani was triumphant. Eph's behavior was an expression of guilt. It made *sense*.

Eugenia told Dani the men had been called away on another "location scout," looking for suitable porticoes and moldings to juxtapose in establishing shots with the too-modern, antiseptic interiors Sforza had rented: another kind of scavenging, with Ephraim in the lead, pointing out the things he'd found on his spree that were too big to carry home. It meant a free lunch, but this preceded by a long walk in the streets with the producer and director. Wexler, trying to cultivate the adjective "birdlike," had taken to flapping his arms madly when Sforza upset him with more talk of replacing Millicent Harkness, or talk of including special "European market" inserts of nude models on divans in *Rose Alley*, to spice the thing up a bit—this launching drizzles of sweat into the air whose parabolas Foche followed, drowsy, with his eyes. Ephraim sagged in the heat.

Though after two hours on the march they moved mostly in step—gunfighters with terrible grudges—they were motley in their particular gaits, at pains to differentiate themselves: Sforza proud and ponderous, scratching his balls as though they housed a great nation; Ephraim pixilated, every step mistook and improvised, reinventing the walk; Foche wide and buoyant; Wexler flailing and petulant. The director was thankful for Bueno: he acted as a damper on Sforza. Here was the faux Jew with his six gold

Stars of David swinging between open fifth and fourth shirt buttons, and then the real one with his Flemish accent, ersatz Spanish name, and Moorish features embalmed in a pale Northern face—no more ostentatious than a ferret. Both Bueno's parents had survived World War II to become tailors in Amsterdam (his mother is with us still, ninety years old, monogramming dressing-gowns in Garamond—she gardens and makes a mean green tea), but Ephraim, when asked, said the Nazis had got them; whereas while Sforza's folks *had* been murdered, he wasn't certain enough about their deaths to advertise it—there were still days he worried that they might just be avoiding him—and so claimed that they'd gone to Zion to plant olive trees. The two canceled each other out. A blessing, said Wexler, and they all thought he was talking about the architecture.

Sforza suggested they stop for food at the Tout Va Bien and bring it in bags to Foche and Bueno's neighborhood dive, to avoid paying a tip. The patronne put up curiously little resistance to this abuse of her hospitality and brought them their bottles serenely, filing away the names of Sforza and Wexler for entry in her punishment ledger. Too tired and hot to squabble, the quartet embarked upon their meal in equivocal good spirits, even when Foche told his employers that they'd soon be obsolete, that in a few years cinema would be made anonymously and by collectives. The mood was only spoiled when Bueno, the worse for drink, spied a bit of manufactured junk (a telephone receiver or rubber ball, a pitch-pipe or parasol handle, abandoned by the café door, kicked in off the street by a customer, or else brought in by Yevgennie, himself a hoarder) and was seized by an unreasoning fear. By all reports he stood on his chair, a housewife screaming at the sight of a mouse, and begged to have it removed. I didn't put it there, he said by way of explanation. It doesn't belong here. It isn't mine. It makes everything around it ridiculous. He wouldn't be consoled and soon exhibited the same terror of the café table, the chairs, his clothing, and even Wexler's spectacles, which he slapped to the floor and nearly ruined. Paternal Foche hurried Eph away under his hot arm, promising to return.

Information as to his whereabouts would be greatly appreciated.

8
Eugenia Sleck

Editing has traditionally been one of the few movie crafts wide open to women, most likely because the position involves little contact with the male-dominated technical crews, but also because it requires manual dexterity rather than brawn and an observant aesthetic eye. Too—thought Eugenia—there was a feminine brand of patience wanted: those fiddly bits of film, strips of repetition, innocuous on their spools, sometimes miles for a single scene. You work to straighten them out, remove the ailing or redundant segments of tract, and fix your stitching so the patch is invisible on the screen. You work to cover the director's blunders, even though in the end *he* gets all the credit for success, and you the blame for failure. There was an analogue with motherhood there. If after twenty years of tinkering your babe turns out a winner, he takes all the praise for himself—self-made. But with him in the gutter, there's no doubt but that *Maman* was the bungler: She did Boy in with her coddling and cuddling. Was too much around or never when needed. Let him sleep like a sword between sire and dam. What could she have been thinking?

What a strange, you'd have to say *avant-garde* sort of thing even
the dullest film was, being in form—as we all know—a series of
incoherent fragments, sorted through and soldered together with
dreamy nonlogic, so that no gaze remains aimless, no gesture redundant: exactly the opposite of life. Each reel is a rope of photo-
graphs, the subject now three days older, now two months younger
than he'll be lower down in the spool: slices of life, quite literally,
high-rise windows, a Zeno's paradox of interminable motion, the
actor forever in the hell of some simple movement, unable to complete it—each step implying an infinite number intervening, an
agony of stasis without the editor's generosity, inserting a blessed
ellipsis.

How had this ever come to seem natural? How, in less than a
century, had we as a species learned to *read* it? Wasn't there something essentially *wrong*, if not immoral, with our being enthralled
by such a pudding of nonsense?

(Unless, the theory goes—and Eugenia was a subscriber—our
minds, in the *process* of consciousness, do much the same thing:
give the illusion of movement and completion by leaving ninety-
nine percent of the world on the cutting-room floor. Old Man
Blake thought so. Had our brains recognized a kindred methodol-
ogy in the syntax of film? Had the editor's function evolved in imi-
tation of the mind's propensity to *cut*?) (And what exactly was lost?
What were *those* feet like, Eugenia wondered—the ones we didn't
get to see? Where did one go to inspect them? How to jimmy the
cutting-room lock? And could you ever get anything *done* again,
once you'd taken a peek? Or were you then, like Achilles—*pauvre
con*, born a gazillion years before the editor—stuck forever trying
to cross the incalculable vastness inside a single inch?)

By the same token, what a dynamic and volatile thing even the dullest little boy was. Even a dud like Filiba Foche, who'd never so much as learned to cry, who never brought friends home for lunch or even played with his toys. Boys weren't cinema, however—a medium where contradictions can be elided—but tiny action paintings of conflict and contradiction: taking in stimuli haphazardly, trying to make a mind from the muck splashed onto their canvases. (Much as the bourgeois in the joke—Eugenia's mother, for instance—stares at a Kandinsky for most of a morning, trying to "get it," and only nods her approval when she finds a squiggle that credibly resembles a poodle in a bowler hat.)

Every day of a boy's childhood is a new opportunity to ruin him. Some chance remark, some fit of motherly temper—some lingering evidence of your own mishandling twenty years before, when you were left with the wrong babysitter overnight, or told a blue story at your bedside by a dissolute Argentinean uncle—coded straight into their cerebellums, carved like dates into their cornerstones. No touch was light enough: you couldn't help but trifle with them. If elevators, motorcars, planes, or calculators were so easily tampered with or as quickly made dangerous, you wouldn't be allowed anywhere near them. There would be a ten-week course just to operate your blender. Exposed wiring was dangerous. How was it all parents weren't paralyzed with dread?

But this was hypocrisy. Eugenia herself, though fretful, was never paralyzed. Her parental worries were speculative, kept under her bed, gathering dust there along with foreign famines, dying alone, and the nuclear holocaust. It was frustration and boredom—with her job, with her son—that brought these misgivings into relief: made her feel a little epistemological, made her wonder where she'd got the chutzpah to engage in such enterprises lightly.

Most days she managed not to think about it. Filiba was her accomplice in this. He didn't provoke. If she was ruining him, he gave no sign. He gave no sign of anything. Though he was *aware*, she figured, and took in everything that went on around him (he had no imagination, far as Eugenia could tell, so his silence could hardly be introspection), she found no changes in him, day to day: just the unbroken surface of his blankness. She'd given birth to furniture. It made her complacent.

And when, inevitably, a new, inexplicable predilection or terror *did* get added to his stockpile (he had no personality, she joked, only preferences), and was bleated from the speaking-end of his teardrop-shaped head (usually in public, she noted, and usually in cramped quarters: the Metro being a favorite, likewise bookshops and bakeries), it was as though the boy was himself *editing* her, her memory, sneaking in scenes of foreshadowing she could only now, in light of his new pronouncement, recall. His tastes didn't evolve over time as most people's did—getting tired of a particular pastry after a surfeit, for instance, or Eugenia being turned off amiable Raoul for a year after she'd given birth (how she regretted it now!)—so much as imply that *it* (a sudden aversion to short-sleeved shirts, say, resulting in freakish, hysterical efforts to lengthen the arms by force, bending his nails back on the unoffending fabric) had *always* been so. Eugenia, for instance, remembering with a shock (from the *newness* of the memory, she'd swear—the scene having the tang of invention, of convenience) the morning an amorous stranger had stroked Filiba's forearm on a vacation beach, or Eugenia's inadvertently leaving the infant naked by an open winter window while answering the telephone—him bluish in his basinet, squalling in the breeze: never again comfortable uncovered.

So in that August of anthills and armored cars, Filiba rolled through the park like a folded sock, pink among the summer pastels, cooking in his cashmere. Eugenia wanting to get back indoors to the shade noticed that the blooms had by some miracle survived the wilting heat and teargas both, and looked now to last until the first frost—but had acquired in mélange a smell like spoiled milk, confirmation of the commonplace that noisome odors are only congruencies of too much sweetness, she concluded. Then she heard a bird whose hateful call was akin to a reel-to-reel rewound at speed. The animal couldn't have been complaining: it was so hot even the bugs were slow. They buzzed you for the privilege of being fanned away. Easy pickings.

She was stuck there until her mother tired of playtime with Filiba: their regular Saturday date. The old woman had become enormous in her retirement, but her circulatory system must have stayed gamine-thin: she was always shivering in her skin, cold even during the dog days. She flourished in the heat, while Filiba seemed oblivious—though he *had* to be suffering, his cheeks red and slick as brick in a hurricane. Eugenia waited on a bench and worked, making pinhole whorls in orange construction paper. A pattern done to her satisfaction, she would slip the paper charily between the plastic sheaves of a portfolio case. She animated them in her spare time, with Raoul running the camera: had finished three minutes of a silent, feature-length adaptation of *The Tenant of Wildfell Hall* after nine years of work. (Eugenia read many books, but to little purpose, for want of a good method.) There had been a time when she tried to coax her husband into going back to still photography. She thought she'd make a pretty model, to Renaissance tastes, and Raoul had a painter's eye. He was killing it with motion, she said. He'd snorted and said white women were too hard to light—did she really want him after a hard day's work to face the same shit at home? He'd abandoned the project after taking a few snaps of Yevgennie in the Brueghely disarray of the corner market, his Miranda forsaken forever dead-center between two potted cyclamens on top of a bookshelf, as though prepped to star in a still life of its own.

Eugenia was a lifelong Parisian, though Hannelore, her mother (née Sleck) was Austrian. The old woman remembered the late empire fondly as a tapering, twenty-tiered wedding cake, with her and her Papa cheerfully bunked down in cream and strawberries on one of the humble lower levels. Her father the draper had been for Hitler when the Germans came, and was well pleased to wed Hannelore to an officer who, during the courtship, had ordered more curtains than there were windows in Vienna, asking Hannelore to model them as though they were gowns or she a transom. Off to Paris then, with her man overseeing Vichy protocol in the film censorship office during the Occupation. The family was billeted in an apartment that had belonged to the aristocracy for generations: after their big dinners the invaders knelt to fondle the cherubs' heads that sprouted from the wainscoting in the front hall, trying to coax those chilly trumpeters' cheeks into divulging the sweet plaster secrets of the beau monde—until one by one they collapsed, releasing sour ferrous smells and blanching the carpet.

In a reversal of the usual story of Occupation *amour fou*—which has the innocent and alluring country girl falling for a Nazi cad and bearing his child only after the liberation, when he's died or gone home, knowing she'll be shaved and beaten as a collaborator—Hannelore had been seduced away from her happy home and two bonnie Blackshirt boy-children by a member of the Resistance (called terrorists, then) who'd been tasked with her abduction by a cell desperate for leverage in negotiations with the Gestapo. He truncheoned her and took her down the back stairs of her hotel, the servants' route, DNA-twisty, for deliveries and laundry and assignations with tradesmen. They repaired to his lair—in the catacombs, of course—where he gagged her and tied her to an old wooden chair stolen from the concierge of his building, informing her that he intended to hold her prisoner until word came that his compatriots had been freed. If they were not, he said, he would presumably have to kill her, and probably in a particularly appalling way, bound to horrify even a Boche. Though the method, he apologized, hadn't been chosen yet, he was sure it would be spectacularly gruesome. His superior officer, he explained, had been an Orientalist at the university before the war. Monsieur Professeur had a particular—not to say peculiar—familiarity with the most lingering and ironic of the executions on record as reserved for those who'd betrayed certain ancient Chinese emperors.

Weeks went by without word. Finally they were rutting hourly on the Roman stone, the parallel slats of her chair snapped and loose beneath her back like the spines of some monstrous corset. Hannelore's limbs were bound tight as ever to the wreckage, his straightjacketed by green oilcloth, only half-removed in his haste, the two of them limbless like serpents in a creek, stippled with splinters, and sounding to the street above—where the walloping of loose chair-wood on wet cobble echoed loudly from every sewer-mouth for miles—like nothing so much as a Brazilian percussion section.

Eugenia called it rape plain and simple—the reason she'd taken her mother's maiden name, despite its own distasteful associa-

tions—and she demanded, especially in her teens, that her mother
recognize and condemn the crime, leave Papa's grave to the weeds,
return his pension checks unopened, and ignore all anniversaries.
But Hannelore just shook her head and smiled, as though rape
like rock and roll had been invented by a generation of faddish
malcontents, beyond Hannelore's comprehension and—anyway—beneath her notice. She said it hadn't been like that at all.
Eugenia had no right to judge and etcetera. It was maddening, the
calm and exactitude with which her mother recalled the scene of
her violation—the rash like *Starry Night* the ropes had given her
wrists, the drip drip of the green water on the brim of Monsieur's
discarded cap—and with what evident relish she related it to every new beau Eugenia brought home for supper. Maddening too
was knowing that though she'd effectively changed sides the day
of her ravishment in the catacombs—never going back to her
scissors-wielding Kommandant and two handsome Youth
Brigadiers in the Faubourg—and though she loved her adopted
country, her less-than-Aryan daughter, and outright half-breed
grandson as devotedly as anyone could want, she had remained
at heart, at the time of her "conversion" and to the end of her life,
as much a Nazi, ideologically, as her father had made her: just a
Nazi with rather heterodox sympathies. Like a mild evangelical
who against her better judgment had married into an atheist clan,
she knew her opinions to be unpopular and tried her best not to
embarrass anyone with them; but she guarded her faith carefully
against erosion, secure and ever-vigilant, certain as a glacier that
though the world had gone another way, hers had been the right,
and that vindication would be forthcoming in the most Wagnerian
manner imaginable—just you wait.

It was too much for Eugenia, then, to see her mother so kind and courteous to the *schwartzers* in the neighborhood—the Nigerians and Arabs, the Cypriots and South Americans—when she herself often felt uncomfortable being the only blanc on a block. Further, her mother always had money in her purse set aside for beggars, chatted with them and bought them cigarettes or sandwiches, while Eugenia found herself crossing the street to avoid them, paid them mostly to keep them away and wanted to peel off her skin after being accosted. Yet Hannelore voted for men who wanted transients put into work camps and immigrants shot for working without visas, while Eugenia was a socialist and would happily have given up her hi-fi and hot-water heater to settle naked in a mud hut if it meant no one else in the world would go wanting.

Hannelore gabbed freely with the few Jews on her rounds, often in German, and could boast a great many friends of that persuasion if pressed to deny her affiliations before a jury (could it be that she foresaw trouble?)—but while strolling with her daughter and grandson she referred without fail to the ringing of every cash register through an open boutique window as someone's "playing the Hebrew Piano," waiting every blessed time for Eugenia to laugh, and then peevish when no laugh was forthcoming, until finally let loose in the park with her grandson, where she surely enjoyed herself more than Filiba ever did, kicking an orange ball around or shuttling him up those grubby monkey bars rain or shine.

In the early days of Raoul's courtship, Hannelore had often consoled herself aloud that though the gentleman was hardly ideal, for obvious reasons, at least you couldn't accuse him of trying to pretend to be a normal European, like your sneakier sort of African. Finally she'd taught herself to keep quiet on the subject

if she didn't want to bear the brunt of Eugenia's temper, which
was loud and cruel and often left her mother simpering. Eugenia
knew Hannelore would happily see Raoul shot, flung in a pit, and
covered with quicklime—yet, had there ever been a kinder, more
generous mother-in-law? She never shrunk from Raoul's embrace
on visits to the Foche household, never turned up her nose at his
cooking, had never once—since the wedding—condescended to
him; while even Eugenia, though loving the galoot as much as
she loved her own legs, was often alarmed in spite of herself at
some new twang revealing itself in his scent or accent, waking up
twice a month with his arm across her belly and wondering at the
strangeness of the man she'd let into her bed.

Of course, Raoul was alien in more ways than one. He saw no
reason not to tease his wife that she'd only married him to bug her
Nazi fossil of a mother—gone xenophile just to rebel. He'd even
hinted that this would be in no way distressing to him. Was it a
joke? Impossible to tell. He was wrong, in any case. Eugenia had
fallen for Raoul when he saw through Hannelore, and without
any prompting. Her other friends and suitors had doted on the
woman. The more Eugenia tried to warn them off, the more they
loved Hannelore in the end—she was so charming and harmless,
a late-autumn pumpkin of a lady. A man who could see right away
what was what—Eugenia's munificence and Hannelore's loath-
someness distinguished instanter, as through a magic glass—
daughter princessy and mother haggish no matter how they'd
painted their faces—was intoxicating to the girl. He was perfect:
held Hannelore at arm's length that first night he'd come over,
when the old woman had made them dinner. Walking to the movies afterward he clapped his shoulders as though from cold and

asked did Gin think Aitch had checked her hand for soot after he'd shook it good-bye just then.

It took until after Filiba was born for Gin to wonder whether canny Raoul had only caught on that what she'd wanted from him, and desperately, was to feel she was a better person than her mother, and whether he had given her this confirmation just to get into her pants. He asked would it upset her if she were correct. Eugenia knew him too well by then to bother being outraged. Raoul had so little malice in him that he couldn't have meant the question as a provocation, and was so lacking in everyday self-consciousness that he wouldn't recognize her distress no matter how blatantly she telegraphed it. He would only go off to sulk with his cat in their bathroom-cum-darkroom if she sued openly for a retraction. When she confessed to seeing the Bueno boy afternoons, after they'd met at the Harkness party, and had scratched her knees kneeling in contrition and all but torn at her hair, Raoul had tried, albeit tearfully, to start a conversation about phrenology. He never so much as raised his voice to Ephraim. Not even when Bueno, abjuring his siesta-time dalliances with Eugenia in favor of playing her ne'er-do-well elder son, took to phoning them four times a day—for help with his *real* girlfriend, or to ask for a loan till payday, or to find out if they knew any antique stores that carried artificial limbs.

Then Filiba would interrupt Bueno's infuriating and humiliating calls to remind Eugenia he'd suddenly never liked chocolate—not once, in his life, on all the occasions she'd seen him eat chocolate, bought it for him, unwrapped it for him, offered it to him as an enticement, had he in fact asked for or enjoyed it, and surely, surely, this had been obvious even then. Where had his mother gotten the idea, he inquired, that chocolate was something he would welcome? She longed to see the ember of comprehension that fear would light in his cow-dull eyes as she throttled him.

Coming home from the park with ten seconds' worth of freshly poked Brontë frames under her arm—after seeing Hannelore deposited at her tenement and a stop at a sweet-shop for Filiba—she found a record spinning on the stereo and Raoul sunk in unseasonable antimacassar on the sofa. Yevgennie sprouted obliquely from his chest. Raoul had anisette on his breath and bad news from Sforza. Another week at least. The Foches did reshoots and patch-ups on army training films for rent money in the meantime: venereal disease, semaphore, wing and tail markings. Eugenia thought she might cry. Raoul scooped Filiba up and lifted him vroom over the paternal stomach, bracing the boy under his arms with his hands, under his thighs with his stocking feet. Yevgennie escaped and tried to interest Eugenia, but she kicked at him and went into the kitchen where there was something boiling over on the range. Raoul was a wonderful cook when he concentrated—it was the only hobby he managed to keep to—but dangerous all the same. He'd stop stirring to wind the clocks or take Eugenia to bed. To dinner parties he'd bring dishes whose only rationalization lay in the ingredients' all being the same color, their names starting with the same letter, or—most memorably—their having been found at stores that didn't sell food.

Some of his meals were so elaborate—the one at the Harkness party took seventy-two hours to prepare—Raoul demanded they be "read" sequentially: each mouthful intended to be taken in strict order, like the notes of a sonata or clues in a *policier*, each dish, unrecognizable in itself, part of a larger, even more confounding "course" (was this the soup? asked Millicent Harkness . . . the cheese? dessert?): food stratified like Aztec architecture. Done

right, he said, the dénouement would leave them all limp with satisfaction. There was no conversation at table, and everyone but
Raoul drank heavily.

Eugenia ended up missing the coup de grâce and kissing
Ephraim Bueno in the coatroom, his erection in cheap gabar-
dine silly between them as they crushed Archie Harkness's coat,
mourning-black—he still grieving for that poor old "secretary"
who'd crossed the channel with him only to die napping in a rented
room right before the riots. It was a senseless lapse (because Raoul
so rarely touched her? because Bueno was spry and feckless?) and
she hated herself for it, not least because no one who'd stayed for
the final course could explain to her what had been served. Wexler
said there'd been too much vanilla, Sforza mentioned some kind of
salsa, and Myrna repented of her vegetarianism because the smell
had been, well, *something*. (Had Raoul drugged them? Was that
how you jimmied the cutting-room lock?)

Raoul would be disgusted with her if she asked how the meal
had ended. He'd never tell. The leftovers were destroyed. She'd
be bringing out trash-bags full of the stuff next morning while
he was away filming bayonets puncturing sandbags at throat and
groin, and wouldn't have the temerity to peek. She went to work
at noon. The freelance editors worked half-shifts on one army
Movieola, and she sat down every day—Filiba in school—on a
seat still warm from her colleague's morning. She never got to
meet him, only see how he'd ruined her work of the previous day.
Male or female, it is difficult to detect a consistent style in the
cumulative work of any editor, for, after all, the most he or she can
possibly do is rearrange existing material and tell a story in the
best possible way.

9
Raoul Foche

He'd seen, he said, a kind of shark, raised by winch out of the ocean. It was on the edge of the desert—this was during his national service—and hung by its tail, ten yards wide, from a gallowslike contraption used for lifting tanks (delicate as eggs) from the bellies of navy boats. The monster dwarfed the hoist, which only held three-quarters of it aloft; its head was crushed sideways on the walkway against the tackle's enormous stanchion, the sturdy metal burbling from the strain. The thing's eyes were each so wide around that its pupils alone were the size of your head, and its nose was disdainfully raised. Its leering mouth, squished open like a toppled drunk's, was biting the ground with sea-tarnished teeth, each incisor long and wide enough to copy Johnson's *Dictionary* onto if you started at the tip and went in a spiral to the gum. Raoul swore he saw no gills in its sides, but that a full set of mammal-brand lungs had tumbled out when his captain cut it open, stem to stern, grasping with both hands a saber's brass handle as he descended in crude hydraulic jerks. He was a picture of gore when he stepped from the cherry picker's basket, the thing's oversize heart like a meteorite steaming in the bowl of his upturned hat. Guts sloshed on the tarmac, the creature's own perplexing lights as well as a stew of fish and seagull and sailor, a mountain that forced the crowd back several paces. The intestines raised a stink like all the zoo cages of the world, but the stomach itself—though its contents were on the ground and attracting gulls—was still lodged inside the hulk, a stubborn wad of pinkish gum the size of a hospital elevator. Some joker, joining in the general high spirits, thought to help dislodge it by taking a potshot into the cavity. The regiment blanched and hit the deck. When someone called an all clear, they crowded around the comedian, the captain yelling and—hands full, unable to gesticulate—bobbling his gruesome cargo in the idiot's face.

While thus engaged, their backs to the exhibition, the stubborn stomach, punctured, jetting fluids, rolled heavily out of its burrow—an avalanche of meat. It cast a shadow over the men closest to the base of the winch, a blot round as a balloon and for a moment as silent, until with an ecclesiastical, gonglike clang it mashed them into the mulch already coating the walk. The hat and heart were dropped in horror and, together, rolled.

I guessed a jeep, an intact jeep it had swallowed whole and like a wedge of fat found impossible to digest or excrete. What luck you got the monster before it grew legs.

But speaking of jeeps, he said, annoyed, had he ever told me about Yevgennie? Not this Yevgennie, of course, not even the one he'd had during the filming of *Rose Alley*, but the first Yevgennie—Yevgennie the First—the parent, along with a pure neighbor Blue, of the kitten who savaged Evelyn Nevers. Of *that* litter only the little prince had survived: rescued by Raoul, who'd raged and shouted, quite out of character, to hide his palming one of the newborns from a box of rolling fur—slipping it squeaking into the pocket of his trousers, where its birth-soft skull was bent into a singular shape by the blade of his house-keys—while the father-in-law, so to speak—a tailor—insisting that he couldn't have six kittens underfoot, blushed and shrunk and apologized all the way to the river . . . but didn't relent.

Yevgennie the First had long since vanished by this time, murdered by superstitious neighbors or stowed away, perhaps, on a ship back home, with a cap on his head and the handle of a little portmanteau clasped in his mouth. Raoul and he had been inseparable since the day Private Foche of the transportation corps had been ordered to drive two colonial brass to a camp at the terminus of a terrible road in the south. This road ran along a string of towns, evacuated or abandoned after heavy skirmishing, where the insurgents had been collecting their own taxes and conscripting hapless village boys pretty as you please. The buildings left standing were so full of holes the settlements flickered like mirages from afar; the whole caboodle rotten now with ghosts and guerrillas both, though marked on the newest maps (and therefore irrefutably) as having been successfully "cleared." The route was known locally as a sort of land-bound Cape of Good Hope: truck axles, starchy uniforms, and sand-filled canteens surfacing up to seventy miles away after an attempted crossing; the debris half-buried, projecting from the sand and weathered to antiquity: scattered by a maelstrom, and all hands lost.

Parked by a rubbled church wall for a piss Raoul heard sounds coming from the trunk. The older men, nervous, asked that he ignore it and they press on. As frightened of staying put as of going ahead, he decided to search the jeep in case of sabotage—saving the trunk for last. He'd look for bombs in the chassis. His superiors rephrased their appeal as an imperative. Raoul inched out from under his machine, staring up through its sparse military innards—the shafts and gears and even the indent of his passengers' rears on the verso of the seats above him all clear as they'd be in a diagram—and held up his hand, index finger extended, asking for one more minute.

The hood was too hot to open. He heard the engine ticking inside as it grew marginally cooler in repose. The trunk made a second skittish sound. He went round reluctantly, the petulant men protesting, the church wobbling, somnolent, in the heat. He opened the trunk. There was something like a body, mummified in an incongruous blue woolen blanket and fetal to fit the space. It had been female and had been young. Raoul reached in and removed her—light and stiff as burnt toast. Too far gone to tell what color she'd been, where she was from, or what precisely had been done to her. It was just as likely that she'd been French or pro-French and brutalized by nationalists not particular how they made their points as a native set upon by bored and bitter Europeans; just as likely she'd been put there expressly to dismay his regiment as hidden in the trunk and forgotten by the men who'd had the jeep out last—soldiers who'd dreamt ever since of losing valuables in a hotel after making love, or transposing the numbers of an important address, and whom he probably saw at mess every morning.

He laid her on the ground. At this slightest of impacts, her teeth came loose, rolling into the dust like dice from a cup. They were rounded every one and red as mahogany. He had a moment's uncertainty then, seeing their resemblance to crude Georgian dentures, whittled in someone's spare time and too casually gummed together. He crouched down by her and looked again. Limbs like cracked broomsticks, hair like straw, the fingers dried and tight as belt-leather and toes hard as ten thimbles; her skin all over like airmail paper: a macabre little manikin. Was the body a fake? Part of a prank? Or had the sun just turned her into sculpture—as it does, in the end, with everything? Raoul's confidence in the body's authenticity—and the concurrent fright in his stomach at the dreadfulness it signified—wavered like the bubble in a spirit level and traveled the length of his scale, up and down, from unqualified faith to livid dismissal and back again so rapidly and so many times that he was exhausted by it. He had to resist the urge to bury the artifact there and then, just to have done with the wondering.

If it was only chance and the harshness of the elements that had cured the body to the point of its resembling a fabrication—faking fakeness so well that even Raoul's compassionate eye could find room to doubt—then this was the last and most cruel of fate's tricks on the girl: this, the only evidence of her ill use and murder, all that remained of her on Earth, preserved in such a way as to undermine itself on sight. She couldn't even rely on witnesses being nicely aghast on her behalf. Her corpse called for verification, not vengeance.

On the other hand, if it *were* some sicko's poupée—a diseased desert Bellmer watching the jeep from the church wall and snickering behind his fingers—well, Raoul would be furious. The ruse would rouse him far more than the honest crime it was meant to suggest. He'd be out for blood.

So he hated the sad little thing, feeling that it was malefic, a fetish object stealing away his will; and he was dreadfully guilty for feeling this way. He collected the teeth and dropped them in his pocket. He stood up, sure his passengers would tell him what to do with the homunculus, but they ignored him, were muttering to one another. Raoul about to show it to them saw movement at his feet and hopped. Having climbed out from where he'd been trapped under the body-object, Yevgennie was introducing himself: affable but hackles raised, striped green with motor oil. The animal had a fabulous disinterest in the body and sat in the dust near her head; his fitful tail swept her faceless, licking around behind him, but his squinty eyes were tranquil, adoring Raoul.

Foche would never know if there was anything else in the car. His superiors climbed into the front seat and took the jeep: food, water, guns, and all. The trunk open and flapping, they sped gracelessly on its blunted tires around the church and back onto what had been the main drag, where a mine sent them up before Raoul could shout hey. There was smoke and noise, but no fire. Yevgennie didn't flinch at the sound. He must have been used to bangs and booms.

Alone then in the desolation, with a French uniform screaming its colors on him and no supplies or shade. But Yevgennie had saved his life. If not for the cat's patient scratching they would all have gone down the same road together. He wore the girl on his back with his belt as a strap and administered kitty into the crook of his arm. It was at most a postponement. He would die far more horribly now, getting back to base. The rebels saved special nastinesses for the pro-French Muslims, or "*Harkis*." They'd assume he was a volunteer, a traitor, and probably cut his earlobes off very slowly with barbed wire. They'd make him wear a necklace of his own fingernails. They wouldn't listen to excuses—and in a sense he had none to give. He'd obeyed his parents when they told him not to protest his mobilization. (His father—who'd volunteered for the frontlines the day war was declared against Hitler and got shot to pieces a few years later in the push ejecting Vichy from Algiers—who walked stiff-kneed, spoke in a monotone, and stuck fruit-shaped magnets to his head to amuse Raoul's school chums on Sunday afternoons—had been granted full French citizenship along with other meretricious Muslims after the German defeat: he'd promptly moved to Paris with wife and son and nothing but his medals to recommend him. Ten years clerking in a tobacco shop had somehow cemented his ferocious conviction that his countrymen should never be allowed to govern themselves. Things are the way they are because that's the way they're supposed to be. He was pleased his son would be lending a hand. Raoul could count on no help from that quarter.) He'd never asked to be stationed elsewhere. He'd never checked whether there was a regulation somewhere prohibiting an immigrant from being sent to war against his own people. For months he'd waddled along happy enough through the rank air of military life, certain the mistake would be found out and he shipped home any day. There was probably another Raoul Foche filing casualty reports in Paris, lucky fucker; soon it would be *him* sweltering and terrified in the desert and our Raoul safe in the city of Atget—happily dallying on his way to work, eyeing new lenses in the dark windows of late-opening camera stores, nursing a sopping butter croissant.

Though he was shuttled back and forth between divisions (each commanding officer too embarrassed to keep him, but none willing to vouch for his unsuitability), he did his full term, waiting all the while for his reprieve. He was taunted for his aloofness—never feeling that what went on really applied to him—called our little Zouave without fail by every new batch of comrades; lucky enough at last to go home before things got *really* bad, but not before so much blood and strangeness had finally made it a matter of indifference. Neither was his case unique: a legless street musician on the Boulevard Saint-Michel told Raoul once that he must be one of God's own favorites to have come through unscathed, then took his discharge papers out from under his robe, ripped and ate them with evident delight, pulling them in conclusion whole and dry from Raoul's front shirt pocket and demanding cigarette money in return.

But did I know that's how he'd met his wife, he asked me—munching my breakfast at the window of a photography store? Unemployed then, taking pictures when he could, doing the occasional shift at the shop where his father ran the register and going to night school when he could afford it. She was nineteen, he was twenty-four; she was walking with friends cutting class and yes he took her picture, his finger slippery enough from his food to nearly miss the trigger. One—not Eugenia—asked could she have a copy. Then all were asking. They were roommates. He got their number.

He slept with them in size order, a happy accident for a man so fascinated with taxonomy. Eugenia was second from last. It was a small apartment, with only two bedrooms—they slept two to one bed, three to the other. With Raoul a fixture it was necessary to concoct new excuses every few days why one's bedmates should go out for the evening, sleep in the kitchen, or stay with their parents (where feasible). When in the fullness of time he moved on to the next in the series he found to his dismay that the ones he'd already been intimate with were just as difficult, dense, and uncomprehending when it came time to shepherd them out of the boudoir as were those who'd yet to be initiated, and whose truculence might therefore stem from legitimate naiveté. Each length of claret-colored carpet in their hall became a landmark in the struggle, each with its own complexities and significance. Could they get the girls out the door? Beyond the dead forsythia? Ten paces past the thin-walled bathroom, with its midden of humiliated pubic hairs and empty unguent bottles?

He couldn't relax until they'd reached the sofa. What bliss when they reached the sofa. Such gouts of protestation he'd had to endure—such a syllabub of stormy, put-upon sighs and spiteful recollections of last minute widgets left *pardon!* at an earlier checkpoint. When they reached the sofa he could be pretty sure of outrunning them to one of the two bedrooms with his lass-of-the-moment and locking the door, if it was the larger, or barricading with the communal mattress the loose, cracked, creaking oblong (with empty peephole instead of knob) opening into the smaller.

It was all too similar to the agony of seeing Archie Harkness off, during Raoul's first and only adventure in adultery: Archie dressing to leave his rented house for the night under the impression that his consent—with regard to the cameraman's diddling his wife—had to be reiterated repeatedly. He was so pleased, he would say, that Millicent had found a friend in Paris. Someone to take her out and show her around while he was off doing tedious actorly things or burying his amanuensis now that the gravediggers weren't striking. The fun they'd have. It would be weeks yet before it got cold, and oh the limpid tenor of the city from a handrail on the autumn Seine. Yes yes, they'd say. The cab is waiting. Don't bother about us, Arch.

But Arch always found a reason to dither on longer—cuff links, tie clip, money belt, revolver—telegraphing his approval all the while as though to friends too slow to get a joke. Everything short of winking at them, Millicent remarked, alone at last with Raoul. Foche was meant to be on a night shoot, making grocery money on the side. It was revenge for Eugenia's own infidelity, he told me: a juvenile and indefensible rationale. Useless too as such, since she never found out. How could he bring himself to tell? It was a tremendous effort for nothing.

Being away from Filiba entire nights was difficult for him—the kid had epic, sheet-ripping nightmares that Eugenia usually snored through—and Raoul found that he couldn't sleep at all without his wife clammy beside him on their futon, the mattress stiff in a shape not unlike a patrician staircase after so many moves to and from third-floor apartments. He was a family man. He couldn't stand to be away from them, unlike Eugenia, who'd made it her hobby to feel constrained: always complaining she never got out of the house except to work or visit in-laws, and who took long walks alone whenever possible—who rhapsodized at length about the diseases Filiba might catch or the risk of crushing invisible Yevgennie's head while walking at night through their clutter to the bathroom. Millicent had intuited this about him immediately: had kept him talking about his son and wife when they shot wardrobe tests together at the Tout Va Bien, subjects he'd have thought would be anathema in the context of flirtation, but were, it turned out, particularly disarming.

It helped too that he was a bit in awe of her. There was something of the command performance in their lovemaking. It was a show, that is, by royal command, and she an audience it wouldn't do to disappoint—even when she was in her cast. Here was a woman who, as a teenager, had bested the formidable Maud Gonne in a knockdown brawl—she the actress who'd so captivated Yeats he nearly lost his mind pining, and who was known as Ireland's Joan of Arc—no pushover even gray and widowed. They blinded two men who tried to separate them, and caved the nose of a third who was only passing and happened to ask what the matter was. Raoul owned LPs of Millie declaiming Shakespeare and Joyce and Irving Berlin and was as shocked at Wexler's coup in hiring the Harknesses as her fans had been at her marriage to the likes of a known pansy like Archie. As for Archie himself, there was history there too: he'd been Raoul's first boss, albeit at several removes. The story is that the man who used to sell Raoul developing fluid had been taken on as an operator by an old professor. This professor, owed a favor by J. Arthur Rank, had been hired as a second-unit director. The shopkeep closed his store and took on distraught Raoul as a focus-puller—together they shot skirmish footage at a gallingly peaceful field in Agincourt for Harkness's adaptation of *Henry V.* When Millicent asked him to lunch, and Archie, pleased, said go on do, Raoul was powerless to refuse.

Sforza's chutzpah in nominating his floozy for the role of Lady Rochester in preference to the older, legitimate actress was a topic Raoul made sure to avoid, certain there'd be a fracas when limping Millicent found out—but aside from this he gossiped freely about cast and crew shenanigans. They were all going stir-crazy: acting out like children left too long alone. Did she know Myrna Krause was probably sleeping with Sforza, though she ran him down as a philistine to anyone who'd listen? That, speaking of which, Wexler had been turned out of the Louvre for having his hand down his pants? That Ephraim's girl had been arrested for burglary? That a foreign investor was sending telegrams day and night, claiming first-hand knowledge of Rochester and demanding they incorporate his lengthy suggestions?

She gave him an ugly, overstated cackle of satisfaction, sometimes at the end, sometimes in the middle of his stories, trying to keep him to the point—the sound solitary as a church bell's at the half hour: "Hee." She must have had other informants as well, since she already knew about Ephraim's "breakdown"; and it was Millicent who'd first told Raoul that his wife was seeing the Hebrew on her walks. He'd been rather flattered by this, assuming that the story was Millicent's way of maneuvering him into bed, until Ephraim and then Eugenia confessed their infidelity a few weeks later.

He'd never experienced such elegance as was on offer at the furnished Harkness house. He longed to screw her in their great purple canopy bed just to feel its flouncing underneath him, but never had the mettle to ask for this dispensation on any of the twelve occasions they found time to dally. Fucking Millicent was something like climbing a marble pillar long as the world: much fortitude was required, and you left frivolity behind with your clothes.

Archie—polite, perverse—sent Eugenia a card, inviting all four Foches for dinner (Yevgennie could play with their foxhound). Eugenia in raptures obliged Raoul to accept, though she was cautious in her excitement. The only words she knew in English were "fair play" and "tommy"; did the Harknesses know enough French that Filiba wouldn't giggle? And why on earth would the Harknesses want them over? Had they done this with all the other crew too? Was it politeness? Were they just moving through the alphabet?

Raoul made noises about having done Archie some favors, about the actor's gratitude for his catering the disastrous welcome party that had forced them out of the hotel Sforza had first booked and into their elegant *maison*. He did his best as they were shown around to hang back from the group, hoping to avoid looking too little amazed at the opulence of the rooms he already knew so well, hauling sleepwalking Filiba to him by a wing of his collar and fussing over the boy's shoes, conveniently unknotted every minute and a half. A row from downstairs—Yevgennie in battle—saved Raoul from seeing Eugenia test the cushiness of Millie's purple yacht-bed, bouncing on it, to Archie's delight, flopping onto her back and saying it felt like a dream.

But how about a chapter on the cat, Raoul asked me, dandling the latest of the line. That would be *charming*.

10
Millicent Kinalty

Her father Rex made a mint in silent Hollywood, getting his start as a farmhand in a Griffith two-reeler before moving quickly up to directing in the days when this was still a matter of being able to shout across a warehouse space, look good in jodhpurs, and bait your leading ladies into quivering histrionics. He had a particular talent—if talent is the word—for turning out safari pictures, where Hottentots happy for the work held hijacked white hunters' wives tied with vines in the shadow of tumescent volcanoes.

When Rex settled down, just after the Great War, selling his house in still-sparse Los Angeles with its private dungeon and seven squiggly swimming pools linked by narrow channels and populated with islands like fat concrete teardrops—spelling at a size only an aviator could read his surname in extravagant cursive (but who would buy a house that had been signed?)—he bought a burnt-out estate in Connemara and left America for good. The local nobs made him Master of the Hounds, hoping to humiliate him and encourage him to leave, but the irony was lost on Rex, who took to hunting with an erotic devotion and contracted rabies from a dog he'd been too sentimental to shoot. He insisted on cosseting it as it died, trying to talk the raving thing into composing itself, as though its convulsions were the result of bad manners. Even after it sunk its teeth hard and far enough into his arm that the punctures had no room to bleed, Rex refused to see the animal hurt and instead had an expert called to help extract it, waiting good-naturedly drunk with his free hand swirling brandy until the motorcar came back from two towns over, bearing an incredulous breeder of spaniels.

Millicent had just turned seven when Rex finally died of it, a lunatic in a camp bed through which he'd drilled by patient scratching two holes for the legs he couldn't be trusted to stand on. He was kept in the foyer, where he'd be more easily attended, and to let Liz Kinalty—who'd married him to get the estate back—sleep in peace upstairs. His groans and recitations reached throughout the reverberant old house anyhow, but it was too much to ask, she said, to have him in the same room. As the bed was on wheels he had limited mobility and often walked his daughter from the front door to the staircase, trundling beside her when she returned from riding lessons, making a din like a bag of marbles dropped and rolling on the parquet.

Millicent worshipped him—Liz said so unfailingly at parties, and word had got back to the girl through the daughters of her mother's friends—but was too young to understand that his peculiarities were not deliberate. Rex's advice being violent and erratic (when Millicent was thrown by a miniature roan he told her frothing to teach all their horses a lesson by feeding them sugar cubes dipped in rat poison), and Liz a confirmed social Darwinist (assured now of her own superiority, having single-handedly undone the damage of her father's dissipation while her brothers eked out livings as dentists and publicans), Millicent couldn't help but come to the conclusion that illness represented above all a *moral* failure, illustrative of a decision on the invalid's part to absent himself from life and lollygag happily at the center of attention. Possessed of a uniquely robust constitution, there were no childhood illnesses forthcoming to put the lie to this supposition (notwithstanding a peculiar mishap, of which see below), and when Rex happened to be buried the same week as her birthday, ruining it decisively, it confirmed this prejudice with a conclusiveness that lasted long into adulthood, when it became clear even to Millicent that sympathy with the sick or dying could be an advantageous sentiment to express.

Mission accomplished, Liz posthumously rehabilitated her disastrous father and hung his portrait in oil over the mantle where dead Rex had had a Rousseau. Mister Kinalty is posed as if surprised at his desk, a handkerchief tied around his head, pen in his raised hand, spinning on a swivel chair to face the painter, alarmed at the observer's intrusion. Past him a curious peahen is pacing a blotter covered with ledger sheets and leaving inky clover-shaped footprints behind. In later years, Millicent noted its similarity to the famous portrait of John Wilmot crowning a diminutive monkey with laurels: the animal is ripping a page from a book and staring up at the leaves dangling over its head, while in Rochester's other hand we see a sheaf of unbound scribbled paper—his poetry, I presume, which in protosamizdat fashion was distributed just so, in manuscript and hand-to-hand around the court (less because of their scandalous content than because publication was beneath him).

It doesn't take much to decipher the Rochester painting. Here is his contempt for reason, for posterity, for mankind, clear as a smirk and in a painting itself a satire of classical portraiture. Granddad's is stickier. Easy enough to assume that the bird is meant to represent his shortcomings as head of the household—bird-brained, flighty—or else, less symbolically, that it's an emblem of the ruin he worried would follow his final retreat into vice (and wild birds did indeed colonize the grounds before Rex came to the rescue with his American money)—but, if so, why a *peahen*? There's a language of birds, same as with flowers: hawks are war, sparrows virtue, pigeons tact, parrots bombast. I can't find any references to the peahen signifying decline. This one looks domesticated, unconcerned. And what was he doing with or to it before "surprised" by the artist? The old man's frustration is evident—unflattering, twisted into a scowl—and the bird makes him even uglier by contrast. Had he dipped it in ink himself? Did he hope to read something in its footprints? Willful eccentricity, Liz called it. She had no truck with symbolism.

Her lover Sylvilla, whom Millicent had been instructed to address as "Auntie," complained that Liz was the sort of mother who'd make a Mozart take a typing degree. This precipitated a row that climaxed with Sylvilla's kidnapping Millicent and taking her to India to prevent her "growing up a boozy dowager who studies genealogy." Sylvilla was older than Liz by a decade or more and had a dreamy air and stammer. She'd spent much of her early childhood in Madras, where her father and now her brothers were hydraulic engineers. She had no particular passion in life and had accomplished so little during her half century on Earth that she'd suggested to Liz that her tombstone proclaim her an "Apostle of Idleness" when she kicked off.

Bathing offshore one morning, and minding Millicent alone,

Sylvilla was saved from toppling into an unfamiliar underwater trench by the sting of something hiding in the sand, startling her into a few minutes' thrashing and thus tipping Millie into said trench in her place. Sylvilla watched in awed dismay as Millie shrank and blurred beyond the invisible precipice a footspan away. In an instant the child was just a pale paramecium wobbling indeterminately blue and distant beneath her.

Sylvilla was poisoned, and the ocean serene as an idol. Limp, lisping with a swollen tongue, she reported Millicent lost and resigned herself to an excruciating demise, which was in any case better than facing Liz after killing her daughter. Sylvilla's family dithered around her; she forbade them to call the consulate doctor, and had already shattered two teeth gritting when a party of native pearl divers arrived at the house with Millie unlikely and indigo in their arms. As though carried off by some submarine condor she'd tangled on a crag by her hair and hung there; they'd been down hardly a minute before seeing and retrieving her—doubly commendable given that they'd been convinced she was a mirage. It was just that sort of thing, the eldest said, that sailors always warned you to ignore.

Only after laying her on the sand and seeing her in the light did they wake from their bemusement and get down to panicking, pumping liters of brine out of a body that looked like it shouldn't hold a pint. Millie lay in nitrogen narcosis for weeks and slept through her mother's arrival (they had all agreed not to send for Liz, but by this time she'd tracked Sylvilla down). The doctors predicted that she'd come around simple from the sea pressure, if at all. Millicent woke to Sylvilla's father declaring with the munificence of a man who had eight children that he'd rather see the girl drowned than a mental deficient. His voice sounded different than she remembered it: its timber distorted, the intonation off, each word missing its proper emphasis, as though he were reading from a page stamped with a square of prose, unpunctuated and all in caps. She laughed then, thinking he was doing an impersonation—she'd seen him do ridiculous things at parties when she'd snuck out of her room at night and stuck her head between the varnished timber of the second-floor balcony, watching Sylvilla and her wizened parents entertaining mad dogs and Englishmen with routines at the piano.

Liz, livid as she'd been since disembarking, held her daughter's hand tight enough to strike it numb, and spoke soothingly if bitterly to the girl. Her voice too sounded false to Millicent, and the girl asked why everyone was talking so funny. Her question softened midway into an irregular singsong whose helpless fluctuations in pitch made Sylvilla's father throw up his hands and storm from the sickroom, fears realized.

It wasn't brain damage. Her cochlea had been mangled by her rapid ascent, and along with them the process by which each frequency taken in by the ear is delivered to the nerve fibers best able to receive it; as though the pattern of holes in a sprinkler head had been bent to favor every rock in a farmyard, leaving the greenery between dry and dying. The world was garbled for her now. Her new manner of speech was an approximation of how she'd been hearing her well-wishers' voices. She had unconsciously and with a kind of genius begun compensating for her head's new tuning, ever-drifting, in order to hear her *own* voice correctly, as she remembered it. Listening to Millicent made many members of the household seasick; likewise, certain harmless and even pleasurable sounds—Bix's trumpet, for one, shrill over Sylvilla's gramophone—now sent Millie into raptures of agony, as though, she said, her brain were being massaged by beetles. She slept out her remaining time in the Orient suffocating under wool earmuffs, Liz fretting that some stray jazz or sleepy finger would get in and rupture Millie once and for all. She dreamt nightly of watching her poppet's bleeding, abundant from each ear like the bilge pumps on the steamer, until the poor dear was fit only for kindling. Liz's indifference to this horrible sight spurred her to greater and more dictatorial acts of solicitude, and it wasn't long before the muffs were pinned to Millie's hair so ingeniously that the least effort to remove them would rip free great gory clumps. Millie's sweat itched and stung under the wool: it was a fantastic effort not to scratch and howl, though the cool of the metal pins against her scalp was for a time something of a comfort.

There were less exotic symptoms. Tinnitus like drops in a cave chamber, frequent headaches, and an impaired concentration that snagged on the least incongruity (Mozzarella on a Spanish dish? An American named Isabella?). The mollusks of her ear canals had almost buckled and for sixty years gave her bouts of churning dizziness, as though she were still and forever poised above that ocean ledge while some cephalopod like a rheumy eye squiggled over her auntie's toe-knuckles.

Millie felt oddly aligned with the bucking of their boat on their journey home. She was the only member of the Kinalty party who wasn't ill regularly and at length over the handrail. Sylvilla had been forgiven. Reduced by the toxin to crone-ish girth and posture she could be found wheeling around the deck under her sunshade, attended by an army of optimistic gigolos. Her girdles she strapped one to another until they made an irregular rubber ring like a whale's lifejacket: she had it thrown heave-ho overboard, commending it to the sea, while the ship's band played "Paddlin'

Madeline Home" and Liz looked on askance with martini and aspirin. Millie missed this and much else besides, locked in the stateroom, where even muffed and with her circulation roaring in her ears the sounds of their carousing battered queerly at her.

Rex's bed like a wheeled war memorial greeted them at the door. Millie jumped onto its stale covers and rode with it shrieking a good ten feet before it hit carpet and bucked her happily over the footboard. She restarted Liz and Sylvilla's argument almost immediately after the latter treated them all to a show at the great Abbey Theatre. Newsboys outside cried of protestors in Limerick burning Hitchcock's version of *Juno and the Paycock*.

Little girl starstruck with stage hocus-pocus. Though the words themselves came through clear, her detuned ears translated the actors' modes of declamation—so long labored over and perfected—into twittering harmonic nonsense. She experienced a pain or pang in the pit of her stomach, a prickliness on her lower arms and neck that she would eventually associate with arousal. She only made the connection years later when an ugly boy at RADA pinched the flesh of her exposed elbow during an acting exercise, the class having been instructed to play the bits of a machine, each improvising a small restricted movement and mechanical sound and repeating them until a halt was called: a wheezing whining assembly line. Millie's chosen movements were stilted, embarrassed. She made the quietest, humblest robot imaginable, pulling her sleeves up when she got too warm; and in fact her first orgasm was aurally induced as well, when a viola line cut through her like cheese-wire during a performance of the "Große Fugue." Once again it was years before she could put a name to what had happened—at the time she'd clutched at Sylvilla's hand and announced after the applause that she'd had some kind of stroke.

Sylvilla, who by then had been through two real if minor ones, smiled in her way and seemed well pleased with her protégé's reaction. If only more folk listened as good as you.

Liz under the ancient misconception that all actresses were whores refused to let Millicent take classes. Sylvilla incited Millie to run away in retaliation when she turned fourteen, her parents' cold war having meanwhile reduced many pieces of Rex's furniture in unused rooms and indeed that poor Rousseau to sticks and rags—wallpaper stripped and hanging in sheets, lamps with broken bulbs jagged under their shades waiting for unwary hands to sniff for their switches—each leaving for the other new disasters to come across in the night. Sylvilla was convinced Millicent was indestructible, as she herself had been at that age, and with the girl certain as well that nothing disagreeable could happen that she didn't bring well-deserved upon herself, she walked into town with a change of clothes and some bread to seek her fortune.

She didn't get pneumonia, because she didn't care to, but Liz did while looking for her, clearing the way for Sylvilla and Millie to move to ruined Dublin and lay siege to its cabarets and playhouses. Millie singing in a revue came to be known as the Galway Siren and drew as many spellbound clackers swooning like Baptists at her accidental arpeggios as she did dismayed, often nauseated purists who paid their ticket price just for the pleasure of booing at her songs and declamations. Sylvilla gave up trying to quiet these critics after the third such show, during which she'd paced up and down the stage in her furs and heels, waving her hands, begging for silence in an accent she was ridiculous enough to think would command respect. This wasn't New York, she concluded. As unusual a voice as Millie's was bound in this town to attract the hisses of conservative ingrates. They wanted even their bawdiest comic songs belted out with the gravitas of a national anthem.

At the seventh show there was violence. It was instigated by a well-to-do woman who declared in the midst of a dramatic recitation that Millicent had charmed her husband away. And there he was, sure enough, glassy-eyed in the gods, his pipe smoldering unattended as enrapt and woozy he made pulp out of his program with wet and nervous hands. Seats were torn from their bolts and thrown, hats trampled, and Millie herself scratched on both cheeks by the thorns in a bouquet an aficionado had meant to fling at her curtain call, but that was commandeered and launched by a skeptic instead.

The next time she went on, Millie was placed for her own protection into an elaborate girl-sized birdcage. Though humiliated and in terrible voice, she squeaked bravely through her bars. While one or two rowdies had returned that night with bricks and noisemakers, raring for another round, the crowd was surprisingly serene. What had placated them was the cage. Millie was an oddity: she belonged in that kind of contraption. It put quotation marks around her. What had upset them most was thinking she was meant to be taken seriously. Now they were free to relax. Even the ones bottle-green with nausea began bringing wives and friends along. It's *meant* to be awful, they explained. It's like being at sea in a storm. It helps if you fix your eyes on one spot—try and keep from looking around. Beckett was a fan; he went to see Millie twice, writing later, in Paris, of the crowds' "enormous scornful smugness," and of Millie's voice "like a drink which made sick in times past and drank again makes sick again but sick now glad harking back to times past" in a notebook with a giraffe on the cover.

After a few years of being toughened by this kind of treatment, Sylvilla brought Millie over for an audition at the Royal Academy. Wispy and eager, she did a scene from *The Old Curiosity Shop* (a Victorian adaptation, by Thomas Blake). She made a quaveringly ingenuous Little Nell. The judges were hypnotized. There will be boys in the class, they cautioned Sylvilla. Boys often try out because they know there will be girls. The classes are coeducational. Sometimes there's touching. Not to worry; Sylvilla would move to London to watch over her ward. Millie meanwhile was in an antechamber sitting on a hard varnished bench, next to Archibald Harkness and his *Richard III*. A teen already balding, he was rehearsing monologues quietly with eyes shut and head inclined poultrylike at the ceiling.

He bought his first packet of condoms on account of her voice and failed spectacularly to deflower her on no less than twelve occasions. Millie was as charmed by his persistence as he was by his own will to persevere; having a reaction to the unearthly sound of her Clytemnestra similar, if less pronounced, to Millie's unique appreciation of late Beethoven. They met in friends' rooms, cars, bathrooms, and cinemas, rubbing at each other ineptly and for the most part without disparagement. (There would be nothing resembling successful coition between the couple until five years into their marriage, at the tail end of the war, after his second spat with the press, on the set of their film about Raleigh and Victoria—the first time he'd managed to shoot in Technicolor [though Mickey Powell and that fucker Olivier hadn't gone wanting for color stock even when London was falling down around their widow's peaks]. Millie had bullied him drunk into removing her clothes and following her instructions, step by step, or else face the coming trial without her support. He obeyed, in part amused—referring to it

as his "rape"—in part repelled, but on the whole perversely determined to prove his virility to her in the most devastating and
memorable manner possible . . . whatever that might mean. Until
then they had taken the trouble to share a room; afterward Millie
moved to the gatehouse. He was deliberately trying to demean
her, she decided. There was only so much she would stand for.
Furious, he quoted her some Rochester when she came back for
her toiletries: *Let the porter and the groom / Things designed for dirty
slaves / Drudge in fair Aurelia's womb / To get supplies for age and
graves.*)

Millicent confessed to Sylvilla that she was in love when her
guardian preparing their bath salts saw marks on her bare stomach, of which Archie was particularly fond. If Sylvilla had taken
the time to have the boy investigated she would have come home
relieved, declaring him quite suitable. Instead she took Millicent
out of school for a tour of Europe and the Americas. They rode a
terrifying airplane from New York to Los Angeles and descending
with bleeding ears Millie thought she saw their craft's reflection
travel along her name spelled out in water and granite beneath
them. She thought of suicide but was never alone long enough
to manage. She willed herself to die and her new pallor tanned
fantastically. She made herself ill despite the mercilessly paradi-
siacal weather and as she lost weight was accosted in the street
by pedophiles or talent scouts wanting her aunt to bring her to
parties. She got voice lessons from an old lady whose specialty
was de-Britishing accents: Millie learned there that if she made
no effort at all to sound "right" to herself, her voice would sound
normal to everyone else. Since this to her approximated the same
ludicrous *sprechgesang* she herself had been accused of affecting, it
made Millie as ill and mystified as her debut audience had been,

and coming out of her own skull the effect was overwhelming. This gave her auditions a sensuous, abstracted air that won the heart of David Selznick, among others, keen to add another high-cheeked nymph to his collection. He was shorter than her and smelled of horse. Orson Welles spilled rum on her at a luau; it meant that her resolve was impure. She must have wanted to fail, wanted to stay alive. She couldn't account for that.

She thanked God for the war when it came and went home immediately, since England and Archie—up on morals charges— both seemed to need her. She held herself personally responsible when her ship was torpedoed and the decrepit Sylvilla went down with it. (The old woman floated long enough to be rescued and died hoeing potatoes in the French countryside during the Occupation.) Millie sodden on the lifeboat saw flashes on the horizon when the other survivors had fallen asleep. Were they harbor lights? U-boats? Something sailors would have known to ignore? But she couldn't, she resolved, take all those poor people down with her. No, those lights would have to be something benign.

11
Archibald Harkness

They saw him go down under a billy club from their second floor balcony and sent their Hungarian concierge into the fray to effect a rescue. She pulled the unconscious Archie by his collar like a husky and in the foyer fed him brandy while outside the kids were heaving stones or tending their wounded or being knocked around by the paramilitary police, everyone spooky by the light of burning cars and crying from the gas. There were sirens, inchoate yells. Parents watching wondered whether they had it in them to defend their homes from scavengers. Children who'd been shushed and confined to their beds rejoiced that they might not have school the next day.

There were more spectators on their porches now than there were demonstrators down on the street. Earlier the block had been crowded with them: jeering at their persecutors, industriously buglike, stripping the street of everything that could be thrown or used to build fortifications. Now the police, giddy at their own efficiency, were taking their time felling the holdouts. The Paris police are equipped with 30,000 billy clubs. They played at musketeers: poking grapey bruises into cheeks and necks with only the tips of their batons, dancing over the rubbled bodies hiccoughing in shock along the curb. When one blow wasn't enough to drop a target, they forgot their pretense to elegance, crumbling hipbones with healthy whacks before resuming their dainty rampage, a black-garbed corps of bad fairies, entrechating through the wreckage in an amateur production of the umpteenth sack of Paris.

The sparse gray hair, his tweed in the heat, the black band bunched high on his arm by panic—these details helped Archie's saviors, a nice bourgeois married couple, mistake him for a professor out supporting his students. He was an old man, blameless, fond of chess; he took the entire *Comédie humaine* every summer to reread at an inherited country cottage. It upset them to see him hurt. He was like a twelfth-century cathedral under a cloud of Flying Fortresses. They needed to feel—for their own sakes—that they'd done something to save a relic.

The students they weren't obliged to help; they hated to see them bleed, of course, of course abhorred the violence of the police, but they knew enough to locate a little satisfaction in their outrage, resenting the students for all the uncertainty they'd brought to the city.

Madlyn and Olivier (Olivier!) could understand resistance, rage, the will to revolt—putting it down to youth, congratulating themselves on having matured—but couldn't really *see* the kids doing anything other than what kids always did, what they themselves had done at university: be idle fornicators, epicures, eremites with pocket money. If this lifestyle was itself part of what the children were protesting against—and Baptiste, their eldest, was out there too, probably having his head caved in—well, did it mean that they and their friends had done wrong to be so placid? Where would they be now if they'd done otherwise? Where did these students *want* to be?

But no, it was impossible to take them seriously. Impossible to imagine them in any other role—to take them out of their motley and dress them in any costume quite as suitable. As droll. This same failure of imagination is what dooms most reform. The radical must make the case that he's been assigned his uniform unjustly—that he's always deserved a better. To say instead that each outfit is just as counterfeit as another brings allegations of self-importance. It's quite natural to want a clown punished for reciting tragic verse, Archie said. Better to stay on as the fool. An old law protects the zany, the half-wit, the loon. You know all about this already. It's why Lear's fool vanishes halfway through. He couldn't survive the king. He'd poke fun at his "Never, Never, Never, Never, Never," and ruin the last act entirely. But how to write him out? The play would buckle under the weight of his death scene. So instead he melts in the storm.

Still, if a wounded girl with enormous eyes had rung their bell, or cried up at their balcony—the police prancing severely in her wake, their helmets blotted with gore like peach stones stripped by giant teeth—Madlyn and Olivier would have opened their door to her, or hoisted her up, no question, despite the danger. But no one *had* come. Their Hungarian had kept the lobby lights out, had soaped the ground-floor windows to discourage all comers. Now Archie had rescued them from their own goodwill, taking up the only extra bed—Baptiste's. No room for anyone else: the sofa wasn't fit for a dog. They were tempted to put an OCCUPÉ sign down by their apartment number, or maybe LA POSITION EST

REMPLIE. They buzzed with delight. Their luck was stupendous. Here was a prize: well dressed, fresh smelling. Who could want a better foundling? He shaved three times a day, bemoaned the absence of a private shower. A gent. A swell. A mensch.

But Archie had a French vocabulary of only about fifty words (the greater part culled from Shakespeare, particularly the meet-cute in Harry 5). He could thank Olivier and Madlyn for their kindness but couldn't explain their mistake when they called him *Notre Professeur*, inquired as to his specialty, asked could he cook anything exotic. He balked at resorting to grunts and gestures, imagining himself pantomiming a crank on a make-believe camera, repeating *Cinéma! Le Cinéma!* while pointing to his splendid face—chin like a prow, ears he could waggle together or consecutively. Steeling himself for this performance, he felt a pit open in his gut, felt his ribs, lungs, and trachea start sinking into it—a terrible anxiety, a paralysis. It was this pit that helped him choose his roles, helped him keep his dignity, and it was rebelling against this imminent buffoonery as it would a cameo in a beach movie. He wasn't like other actors he had known: he didn't care to please or play the fool. In fact, the prospect horrified him. He was *not* a fool. He made them a fondue.

Archie hadn't done impressions at school, never went in for comedy revues. He could play comic roles—excelled at them, he thought—but they were performances consistent with a comic milieu: of a piece with the rest of the show, not the least bit obtrusive, in no way degrading. Even slapstick was dandy by him, though he wouldn't do the sort that got him messy (wet was acceptable, but nothing viscous). He could fall better than anyone he knew, in the middle of a sentence crumble like an empty suit and bounce his dead-weight head off the floor without pausing for breath. He'd done this all the time in the old days, a party trick, before he married. (Millie had strengthened his already overdeveloped sense of shame.) It caused enormous consternation—gasps, calls for a doctor—before the laughs came: folks recognizing that Archie's side of their conversation was still ongoing from the carpet, meek and unhurried.

This laughter was acceptable. It was due first to incongruence—the root of all pure humor—and then sustained in admiration: a communicative sound, like a sigh. It signified that they understood. He was a willing engineer persuading an audience to take part in a brief exchange: trading them something for their complicity. They shared the joke; it was at no one's expense. Here was moral comedy. A blueprint for the ideal revolution.

First they took his clothing, Madlyn promising to wash and iron them herself. Archie was left Baptiste's green silk pajamas. He had a pair just like them at home; said, I have a pair just like them at home. The prodigal's mattress was light and thin enough that Madlyn could pick it up with one hand and stuff it into its sheet like a check into an envelope. It was made from a yellow foam that unkinked with obscene little shrugs inside the linen and rested level on an irregular plank probably stolen from a construction site in place of a box spring. At night Archie thought he could feel the stuff reaching into his skin, through the sheet, like the invisible filaments in fiberglass. He dreamt more than once of waking up with the thing attached to his back, sagging behind his pajamas like a polite shell. They called it the pouf and Archie laughed. The poof on the pouf.

He woke up reduced to schoolboyhood by the miniature room, the hard bed, the smell of soap and sperm. I've been getting threatening letters from his authorized biographer. His wound was huge and brittle like a pastry on his head; it had flaked a furry mound of crumbs red into his dyed hair and onto his pillow. His aching now in tune with the astonished smacking and popping of his joints, the sight of his black armband crumpled on Baptiste's armoire, and the memory—still unfamiliar—of its implications: these things served to age him up to and then past his proper tally, leaving him shivering as though it were November and he a doddering ancient of days.

He deferred parting Baptiste's elaborately tied curtains. They hung from hooks rather than a rod and met in a thick adorable bow at the top of the window, level with Archie's Adam's apple—making a gift of the street, he theorized. As on the morning after a blizzard, he preferred to have his coffee and read the paper before seeing how deeply he'd been buried. He half figured on there being burning shells of buildings out there, Boschian corpse heaps cooking in the sun; figured, in fact, on living out a heartbreaking end-of-civilization scenario with Madlyn and Olivier, the three of them unable to communicate but unfailingly polite, using up the last of their food on sophisticated dishes, never mentioning the backed-up toilet or the smell of carrion or the front door splintering under their famished neighbors' fists. Archie wondered whether being famous would be worth anything with Paris in ruins. Would a tribal chief be more likely to share his dog-steak with a star than a nobody? Put quantitatively, Archie had no skills whatsoever aside from oratory and an offhand genius for grooming himself without mirror or brush. Alone, he would certainly die.

In the bourgeois apocalypse film he was imagining, the movie star would merit a particularly gruesome death for presuming that he could trade on his fame after the fall. But it's a fact—isn't it?—that people deal more kindly with familiar faces. Strangers are enemies, by definition, but show business makes it possible for folk to become comfortable with you without your ever meeting them. Note that acute humiliation can't be experienced in front of intimates: we make a habit of assuming that their ways of seeing the world are similar to our own, are known quantities, and therefore benign. Paradoxically, strangers' opinions matter more to us because they aren't so easily parsed. They threaten to put us in an alien light. A trimming away of such antinomian viewpoints comes as a wonderful, if disgraceful, liberation. One can imagine being relieved to see a stranger die because the mind finds it easeful to be rid of the burden of accounting for their opinion. It could well be, then, that the will toward fame—toward exhibiting oneself—is not itself the product of a venal culture, but a needful evolutionary function, like a distaste for septic odors, or a tendency to dote on round faces with large eyes. A way of preserving the species. If civilization was evolving toward a general exposure and celebrity, as he'd often heard it said, perhaps this would after all result in a more reverent, respectful world: with no strangers, and thus no anxiety. By this logic, his life could very well depend on his box office. Maybe everything he'd done in his career was actually vital to his continued survival. He wouldn't mind the end of the world so much if it brought with it this sweet validation.

His clothing had been left for him while he slept. Ruined, bleached with pink gibberish constellations, they'd been stacked, folded with conspicuous precision on a wicker chair sporting enough clumps of Baptiste's hair for a witch or criminologist to do a world of harm. Archie had left his shoes, as was his custom—and in defiance of the precepts of an old Manx nanny—facing different directions on the floor by the bed, parallel with the position of his crotch while he slept. They'd encroached a heel and toe's breadth respectively into the outermost orbit of an oval throw rug, green and white in rings to a central lime singularity that the left had pointed toward like a diver. This morning, however, they were gone. He bent to look for them under the bed, and cried out finding a large-eyed face vibrating there in silence on a moss of Baptiste's bunched socks and love letters.

The girl slid out, frictionless as a dust mop, mainly naked in a prepubescent's nightgown. Backing now on bare feet to the window, she held both shoes to her chest, properly arranged with both toes aimed to her chin. Archie's first thought was to twist his property out of her hands, certain her fingers would give way like fruit stems—that like fruit stems they *intended* to give way—but a car horn sounded, making her fearless, and she rushed past him calling for *Maman*. He parted the curtains then, taking in with a little dismay the quotidian street scene below. He chided himself. It had been silly to think only he and his hosts would carry on playing at civilization after the end of the world. Of course everyone else would want to play too.

Dressed, and with his shoes newly shined (or only painted, as he suspected, and with something like India ink instead of polish, leaving voluptuous blue footprints like dance instructions in his wake), he presented himself in the kitchen, where his bed elf was naked in the sink, a peeled succulent, being bathed by her mother. He asked after his script. Fat as a bible, he'd nonetheless managed to roll it up and fit it into an inside pocket, still scented by the leavings of a Victory cigarette—souvenir of a pack bummed off a GI pretty enough to attract sniper fire at the retaking of Paris—and he'd forgotten to rescue it before letting Madlyn take his jacket. He wondered did he have a concussion, whether this would keep him from learning his lines. He wondered if Madlyn the inept housewife (actually a typist) had bleached Myrna's opus along with the jacket by way of cleaning off his blood: forgetting to turn out the pockets before dunking the lot into what was probably the family mop bucket. It would be a wonderful excuse for not knowing the part, and he suspected Krause would be pleased at seeing her work reduced by misadventure to a sheaf of bound blank lightweight cotton bond.

What a relief to pretend that he didn't have to do the Rochester movie—even for a minute! Millie had begged him to take the part. The writing was "cod-Shakespearean," perfect for Archie—no loss of dignity, a tidy sum (below his usual, but better than selling the house), and a break from his reputation as a fogey classicist: Archibald Harkness willing to be a little dangerous, to hobnob with the longhair set. They would probably use pop music on the soundtrack.

His stomach had started acting up the instant he'd met his producer and costars. Some hardly spoke English. Coming from Italy, Sforza had no qualms about shooting without sync sound: dubbing over Italian or French or even German actors with Oxford English in post-production. He'd even asked if Archie would mind doing some of this dubbing himself, voice Dryden (the actor was Czech), King Charles (Spanish), as well as a chorus of whores and coffee-house wits providing gossip and exposition, à la *The Magnificent Ambersons*, Sforza little knowing or caring what kind of ridicule this practice would call down from the Anglophone critics on his illustrious star and nascent auteur both. Doomsday would have taken care of *that* problem as well.

(A lovely section of this sound work still exists, in pristine condition, something like a *Hörspiel*, with Archie taking on several roles, including a number of old women: chatting with himself, for instance, as though it were pressing news, about Rochester's refusal, due to "a certain distemper," to duel with his fellow poet and courtier Lord "All-Pride" Mulgrave, who was under the impression that Rochester was making insulting remarks about him around the court ["He had said something of me, which, according to his custom, was very malicious"—a self-fulfilling prophesy Rochester was to consummate in due time: *His starved fancy is compelled to rake / Among the excrements of others' wit / To make a stinking meal of what they shit . . .*].)

It was one of the reasons he kept returning to Madlyn and Olivier's little flat. Over the months of the "phony war," as he called it, waiting for the May fracas to die down and for shooting to start, he would slip away from his affluent rental at every opportunity and go down to Madlyn and Olivier's place, letting poor Millie—convalescing, covered in radiant spider-bite bruises down her back where the boots had dug in—think he'd found a new lover (and insulted that she was so easily persuaded—he was in mourning, for Heaven's sake!), taking circuitous routes and backtracking often, as he imagined a conspirator might do, sometimes getting lost and having to follow the polestar back to a tourist landmark like his old nanny taught him. All this to relive that morning of trauma and indeterminacy, to forget that he was being obliged to play a man who hadn't lived to be half his age, forget the ghoulish yogurt-and-glitter makeup they would slop on his face to fake it. His hosts never asked their *professeur* where he'd been or why he'd come back, never thought twice about letting him nap or stay the night in what was now his bed, his room. Their daily routines opened to accommodate him. Madlyn had even begun knitting a sweater for Archie, but she only thought of it when he was in attendance. Her needles clacking like panicked telegraphers through the night stood as a metonym to him for the at once soothing and exasperating environment of the apartment, to which he was now hopelessly addicted. At the end of every visit, Madlyn made him stand and try the sweater on in pieces over his clothes, the sleeves never getting attached to the trunk or the collar entirely pleated. The little girl would steal pieces of the dismembered sweater and run around in circles, the fabric spinnaker fluttering. She would scale Archie the alp without warning or permission, pinching and scraping her way to his head, from where she'd want a ride around the room, her demands shrill and saccharine, her hairless weight on his neck hot as tar.

Madlyn left the discipline to Olivier, but Olivier was usually out: he worked punching program cards for the vast computers intended to take over tabulating the city census, and as 1969 approached he worked progressively more overtime. He told Archie over dinner one night—*Notre Professeur* understanding about a third of the story, literally one word out of every three, and this usually a preposition—that a company wag had found an old player piano at a junk shop and set it up in the company foyer, a mocking memento mori for the professional puncher of holes, it was said, or else (and Olivier favored this interpretation) a reminder that the future is as mortal as the past, that—being potential—it dies many more deaths, and is in the end more profoundly forgotten, than the farthest antiquity. We recognize ourselves, he said, in objects from early civilizations, however peculiar their design: sculptures, scalpels, coins. It's what we build for the future, for eventualities that never come to pass, that remains the more alien. We're in a hurry to get rid of such things, though they persist all around us. They make us itch. If it weren't for the anoraks, collectors, and cultists—already remote and out of step with the world—working to preserve or at least draw our attention to them, these leftovers would be as deeply buried as the gospels that mention the prophet excusing himself for a piss.

Archie would have been happy to know there were thoughts in Olivier's sandy head, but would have been happier still to have this reasoning at his disposal. Wasn't this exactly what Wexler and Krause—and Sforza—were doing? To celebrate a sordid, vicious, puffed-up misanthrope, however witty, however attractive, and moreover to commemorate his brutality toward his better— Dryden, a great man, a man who wrote to live, not out of conceit, the poet-chronicler of his age—this was the act of a perverse hobbyist, determined to see history in the light of its grubbiest culs-de-sac. Why dwell on the muddy pools and drains rather than the grand, pure flow of the river? It was willful ugliness—teratology: the science of monsters and prodigies. Really, Archie wanted no part of it.

We can conjecture, however, based on the trajectory of Archie's career—or what remained of it—that despite their miscommunications, Madlyn and Olivier and Paris all had a profound effect on Archibald Harkness. After the disaster of *Rose Alley*, he conceived an original project, a vehicle for connecting with the younger generation, and went on to write, direct, and finance it himself—ignoring for once that pit in his stomach, telling himself it was time to take a chance.

It's the story of an old professor, in black and white. He's fired after decades of loyal and unremarkable service. His wife leaves him and takes the house. His students find him wandering the streets. They are young and pretty and spend much of their time on body painting and singing. At first the professor is stodgy, he tries to organize them, help with managing their university grant monies, help them pass their finals and get good jobs. Eventually their joie de vivre and promiscuity wear him down. The center-piece of the film is its turning, *Oz*-like, to bright, oversaturated color. The professor learns to see the world as they do during a long and unlikely acid trip. The movie becomes a confusing phantasmagoria of special effects and trick shots, animal masks and pop music. Converted, he leads a parade of students down to the university, which is painted in riotous colors and transformed—magically, with a wave of his cane and an optical "wipe"—into a psychedelic utopia, with blobs of fluorescent purple and yellow defacing the severe granite facade. The other old men and women are converted and shuck their clothes. A crane shot shows them frolicking on the grass.

It ruined him, and Archie died too soon to see its renaissance on the schlock nostalgia circuit. I am lobbying for its release on home video.

12
Poet Squab

On the 18th instant in the evening, Mr. Dryden, the great poet, was set upon in Rose-street, Covent Garden, by three persons who called him rogue and son of a whore, knocked him down and dangerously wounded him, but upon his crying out murder they made their escape. It is conceived they had their pay beforehand, and designed not to rob him, but to execute on him some *feminine* if not *popish* vengeance. He had come from Will's Coffeehouse, and we can surmise that the taste of blood was buried in his mouth under the relentless dunglike bitterness of that establishment's all-day brew, that though he'd been left to steep in a puddle too piquant to be rainwater, his nose, with its new topography of sharp red peaks and molten lakes, still spoke (to his relief) of nothing but shag tobacco—a substance easily confused with coffee grounds by the light of Will's oily tallow, leading, the Laureate supposed, to frequent substitutions.

Wexler wouldn't let Myrna put money into the gas heater, nor would he spend what they'd saved, letting the change pile up in a

sock he kept under his pillow. Swung, it would cave your head right
in—Dryden limped for the rest of his life. Wexler's idea was that
the cast and crew would find out as much as they could about their
characters and the background of the film. Read Rochester and
Dryden. Write their own dialogue. Even the ones who couldn't
speak English. Myrna would be unnecessary. Everyone would be
unnecessary. There wouldn't be any need for props or sets. Which
they didn't really have anyway. The only necessary thing would be
an organizing intelligence. Wexler's. And the camera. The characters would relate directly to this eye. They would make their
own context. It would be impossible for a modern audience not
to see a resonance with what had been happening in the streets.
With what was happening in the world. It would be a documentary fiction. A dialectical fiction. With fucking. (Simulated.)

Mr. Dryden never served in the army, never fought a duel. He
knew violence only in the sense that it is ambient and pervasive
in city life. He came from the landed gentry, but writing was his
trade: he lived from it. If he worked in wood or stone or glass we
would call him an honest craftsman. Take away the system of patronage that guaranteed his daily bread and we'd recognize a contemporary . . . not a poet, but a columnist, critic, or historian. His
name was ubiquitous. His plays were successful. He repopularized
Shakespeare, though in new versions by himself, toning down the
excesses and "native intelligence" of that burly country boy. He
was both loquacious and shy. Panic brought out the best in him:
the rhetoric he commanded in flattering his noble patrons rose to
heights of such sublime preposterousness that much of his poetry
is muted and pusillanimous by comparison. He was, if nothing
else, a great survivor.

Rochester, however, who collected poets and actresses, was

good at everything except survival. Attracted to talent, attracted just as much to success, he sent Dryden guarded praise, gave him money, and recommended a play of his to King Charles. Dryden dedicated the published version to Rochester as a result. Privately he considered the Earl a talented dilettante, but in print was free with tricky praise for R's own—unprintable—verse. I have so much of self-interest as to be content with reading some papers of your verses, he wrote, without desiring you should proceed to a scene, or play, with the common prudence of those who are worsted in a duel, and declare they are satisfied when they are first wounded. Your Lordship has but another step to make, and from the patron of wit, you may become its tyrant, and oppress our little reputations with more ease than you now protect them. And, in a letter: I find it is not for me to contend in any way with your Lordship, who can write better on the meanest subject than I can on the best.

Later, after they had quarreled, Rochester claimed to have always considered Dryden a kind of performing animal, something mean and ugly that had been trained to make music. Wilmot was the Laureate's opposite number in every respect. In a course of drunken gaiety and gross sensuality, with intervals of study perhaps yet more criminal, with an avowed contempt of all decency and order, a total disregard to every moral, and a resolute denial of every reader's obligation, he lived worthless and useless, till, at the age of one and thirty, he had exhausted the fund of life, and reduced himself to a state of weakness and decay—so the Dryden-booster Dr. Johnson. Paradoxically—being a nobleman, wit, and dandy—Rochester had seen bloodshed at an early age. He didn't have the luxury of staying a civilian in wartime, nor could he avoid the regular, petty contests of honor that were the only real check on his and his peers' behavior at court. Barely twenty, he saw a friend's head taken off by a cannonball during a failed raid on some Dutch trading ships. The two had made a pact before the battle: if either died, he would do his best to visit the survivor and give him the skinny on the afterlife. That this friend never called on the young Earl, head in hand, and that Rochester thenceforth devoted himself to irony and nihilism, is a biographer's trap *par excellence*, I think.

So, poetry was not Rochester's profession, but the best application of his wit. For a nobleman, poetry was a calling card, an adjunct to an audacious reputation; and to be witty was a wonderful safeguard, endearing you to the King (when it didn't enrage him—though even rage could turn ironical in a man like Charles II). Rochester was known in his lifetime as a sinner first, satirist second. If anything, his poetry was a consequence of his character, censorious and profligate by turns—like the claws or antlers of an animal. (Are we supposed to be praising people for things they can't help?)

Rochester could have kept to the country, led a quiet life, and been comfortable enough without writing a word—or no more than the next man, verse being endemic during the Restoration. That he considered himself a poet—however frivolously—is demonstrated by the enmity that sprung up between himself and Dryden. That he was *considered* a poet is clear from the testimonials of those who, after his death, had the temerity to praise his work (Aphra Behn: *He was but lent this duller World t'improve In all the charms of Poetry and Love; Both were his gift, which freely he bestow'd, And like a God, dealt to the wond'ring Crowd.* Marvell: *He was the best English satirist and had the right vein.* Pepys: *As he is past writing any more so bad in one sense, so I despair of any man surviving him to write so good in another.* Great blurbs.) Though his own out-put was minuscule, and too lewd and scabrous for publication or acclaim, it was intolerable for Rochester to see a protégé be con-sidered his superior. Likewise, it was disagreeable for the protégé to see his patron as a competitor.

What began as a simmering rivalry—kept below the boil by the flattery that passed between the middle-aged poet and his young patron, who wouldn't live to see middle age—became open hostility when Rochester caused a mediocrity named Crowne (ac-tually a friend of Dryden's, and therefore exceptionally inconve-nienced by the honor) to receive a royal commission in Dryden's place: to write a masque for performance at Whitehall, tradition-ally the Laureate's privilege. Dryden was stung. He successfully courted John Sheffield, Earl of Mulgrave—perpetrator of the rumors of Rochester's cowardice, and just the sort of talentless manqué Wilmot was not—and dedicated his next play to this new patron. Ten years earlier, the two earls having agreed to duel on horseback, Mulgrave arrived badly mounted and sought to fight on foot. Rochester told me, wrote Mulgrave, he was so weak with a distemper that he found himself unfit to fight at all in any way, much less a-foot. My anger against him being quite over, because I was satisfied that he never spoke those words I resented, I took the liberty of representing what a ridiculous story it would make if we returned without fighting, and therefore advised him for both our sakes, especially for his own, to consider better of it, since I must be obliged in my own defense to lay the fault on him by telling the truth of the matter. His answer was that he submitted to it. This entirely ruined his reputation as to courage (of which I was really sorry to be the occasion) tho' nobody had still a greater as to wit.

Rochester responded to Dryden's defection with his "Allusion to Horace," sent anonymously from his country retreat to the little court of wits at Will's. Given Rochester's character, one can only marvel at its restraint. It begins, *Well sir, 'tis granted I said Dryden's rhymes / Were stol'n, unequal, nay dull many times. / What foolish patron is there found of his / So blindly partial to deny me this?*, and moves in due course to

> Dryden in vain tried this nice way of wit
> For he to be a tearing blade thought fit,
> To give the ladies a dry bawdy bob,
> And thus he got the name of Poet Squab.
> But to be just, 'twill to his praise be found,
> His excellencies more than faults abound,
> Nor dare I from his sacred temples tear
> That laurel which he best deserves to wear.

A dry bob is what we'd call a dry hump ("coition without emission"). A variant has Dryden uselessly shouting "Cunt!" at intervals—using profanity to get laughs when his banter falls short. "Poet Squab" stuck as a nickname, outliving Rochester, and though the satire acknowledges Dryden's fussy genius more than once, Squab himself saw it as an assault, striking as it did at his self-image more than his talent. Meticulous, solemn, plump and graying, he couldn't compete with the young rakehells of the court, to whom he was continually obliged to make obeisance and—worst of all—to flatter their verse. (We who write, he wrote, if we want the talent, yet have the excuse that we do it for a poor subsistence; but what can be urg'd in their defense, who not having the Vocation of Poverty to scribble, out of mere wantonness take pains to make themselves ridiculous?) In front of the actresses and statesmen Rochester and his imitators were so adept at impressing, Dryden would have felt terribly out of place: with the actors rehearsing one of his plays, he was in a position of authority, and could thus be charming and garrulous. With powerful men too, he knew where he stood, and so had no difficulty humoring them, taking care never to seem particularly clever when it might show up a person who could be of use. In the free-for-all of actual, unstructured social interaction, however, he was hopeless. Open and public competition paralyzed him. Squab took refuge in craftsmanship: the regular and workmanlike way he sat down to his writing each day, composing, commenting, translating, transposing . . . hours on end, in a set and obdurate schedule—an artisan, not a dilettante. He began work at eight sharp and wouldn't so much as speak to his wife until he'd counted out his allotment of words. If he caught himself whistling or humming, the punishment would be to skip lunch. A single note of music at the wrong moment could empty his mind for an entire day. He forbade family and friends alike to ask him how his work was going, even when he was clearly pleased with himself and dying to talk about his progress in one project or another—and even though he would become grumpy and sullen when something had just been finished and no one thought to congratulate him. But even this hard-earned bit of vanity—that he was a serious worker—was sniffed out by Rochester in his "Allusion," for

> Five hundred verses every morning writ
> Proves you no more a poet than a wit.

And, privately, to his friend Savile (three years before the attack): You write me word that I'm out of favor with a certain poet, whom I have ever admired for the disproportion of him and his attributes. He is a rarity which I cannot but be fond of, as one would

be of a hog that could fiddle, or a singing owl. If he falls upon
me at the blunt, which is his very good weapon in wit, I will for-
give him if you please and leave the repartee to Black Will with a
cudgel.

When Mulgrave published a satire of his own, attacking
Rochester, among others, and word circulated that the Laureate
had had a hand in its composition, Black Will, strangely enough,
tracked Squab down—and pain, like that note of music he so
dreaded, emptied the Laureate's mind, until he found himself worrying away at the sensation in his thoughts in much the same way
he would worry away at his work. The new had to be rehearsed
and repeated until it was no longer a threat. Until it had been
digested and couldn't be distinguished from a concept he himself
had authored. This was as true for a truncheon as an idea.

He blew his nose and it made a red butterfly in his handkerchief. Did he suspect Rochester immediately, or did he think he'd
just been mugged? They took his purse. What else did they take?
He probably had nice shoes. He might have had some jewelry.
He sat hours, half awake, before someone saw him and came to
help. He'd dragged himself by his fingers and knees to a stoop
under a cloth awning, to get out of the drizzle. Gravel and grain
and horseshit had collected under his thick, overlong fingernails.
Or no—people were more solicitous then: someone sounded the
alarm and helped him to shelter right away. Offered him something to drink. What would they have offered him? Squab almost
wished he'd been left where he fell. He hated to be seen suffering.
He tried to joke with the people who came to his aid, speaking
too quickly because of the pain, making light of his situation, but
he had to interrupt himself, hissing through his teeth, groaning.
Eventually he cursed at them all and told them to stop bothering

him with questions. He rocked back and forth, cradling first one knee, then the other, and so gruesome no one knew where exactly he'd been hurt. And if we leave aside the facts of the matter, which tell us that Rochester was already keeping to his country estate, was already going blind and was mostly lame when Dryden was attacked, it's tempting to put him at the scene—that's how a movie would do it. In disguise—perhaps revisiting his most famous role, that of the great Italian mountebank Alexander Bendo, whom the Earl had invented during one of his regular periods of disgrace . . . sneaking back into London and setting himself up as the most popular (and effective!) quack, astrologer, dentist, beautician, and ladies' confidante in town. (It is fit, he advertised, though that I assure you of great secrecy as well as care in diseases, where it is requisite, whether venereal or others, as some peculiar to women—the green sickness, weaknesses, inflammations, or obstructions in the stomach, veins, liver, spleen, &c. [for I would put no word in my bill that bears any unclean sound; it is enough that I make myself understood; I have seen physician's bills as bawdy as *Aretine's Dialogues*, which no man that walks warily before God can approve of]—but I cure all suffocations in those parts producing fits of the mother, convulsions, nocturnal inquietudes, and other strange accidents not fit to be set down here, persuading young women very often that their hearts are like to break for love, when God knows the distemper lies far enough from that place.)

Rochester was considered a master of disguise and a brilliant mimic—taking pleasure to disguise himself as a porter, or as a beggar, and, according to a contemporary commentator, at other times, merely for diversion, would go about in odd shapes in which he acted his part so naturally that even those who were in on the

secret, and saw him in these shapes, could perceive nothing by
which he might be discovered—but then, those were murky days,
and mistakes were easy to make. (Spectators do not find what they
desire; they desire what they find.) In a putty nose, then, dragging
Dryden out of the street and under shelter, asking him in a ridiculous Chico Marx accent what had happened, and Squab begging
for silence while he was in such agony.

What was galling, the hobbled Squab considered, most galling
about the attack, was that it represented an attempt by Rochester
(*of course* he suspected!) to place Dryden the Laureate in the context of low comedy. It was an act of literary criticism. This was
life as seen in a Rochester poem. He even had an erection. Why
in God's name did he have an erection? First one in ages, too.
Impotence or premature ejaculation are often attributed to characters in movies that the filmmakers want to seem ineffective,
mildly repugnant, even villainous. No, this was nothing more or
less than a reveling in cruelty and ugliness. *Yeah, it's-a shoo ugly,
Boss.* And Squab was singularly ill-equipped to parse the statement
Rochester had made—here, of all places, in Rose Alley, where
the paupers who'd died from the plague had been stacked in grim
pyramids, then exhumed and stacked again, trailing their hair and
clothing. Their final resting places were accidentally plowed up
by workmen digging foundations for new houses, as a contemporary journalist tells us, for they were thrown all together into
a deep pit, dug on purpose, which now is to be known in that it
is not built on, but is a passage to another house at the upper end
of Rose-alley, just against the door of a meetinghouse which has
been built there many years since . . . There lie the bones and remains of near two thousand bodies, carried by the dead carts to
their grave in that one year—1666—and, well, it was exactly the
sort of setting Rochester would favor for this little dramalette. As

Squab had said of him: not knowing what it is to praise, but only to throw down and disgrace the subject took up, excepting when that subject is insult itself, the mean, the grubby, the abject—in short, to praise negation itself, which is no kind of praise, and is the very opposite of a prayer.

But Myrna, watching from the wings, making sandwiches for the crew, seeing all these hesitations as to approach, and seeing too that her script would be the first casualty no matter how their movie was made, asked, who's the more readable now, Squab or Rochester? Dryden was a talent, certainly, but his poems are a graveyard for academics. Rochester, though, is immediately explicable: contemporary as a dirty limerick. (But is there such a thing as a *brilliant* limerick?) That he had only sex, death, and derision on his mind in no way lessens his stature. History grinds down commonplaces—"time with its fine sandpaper"—but the grotesque is a timeless verity. When there are no more cars or phones, no amusements parks or summer camps, no neon tubes or hairspray, no record players or cinemas, when as many years have passed between you and your audience as between us and the reign of Charles II—

But Wexler didn't believe for a second—and didn't believe that Myrna believed—that there would be a civilization around in 2269 that cared about film, or art, or anything more (or less) complex than survival. And, you know, grotesquery wasn't the problem so much as making a fool of oneself. He hadn't signed on to make a titty flick. There would be some awful comeuppance. The best tribute to Rochester, author of "Upon Nothing"—

> The great man's gratitude to his best friend,
> King's promises, whore's vows, towards thee they bend,
> Flow swiftly to thee, and in thee never end.

—would be a film that began in strict and regulated intention and then lost itself in dissolution and uncertainty. A shrug. The best tribute to Dryden would be to put in everything that Sforza wanted, but try to incorporate these elements with some modicum of style—to let them generate possibilities rather than close them off. This after weeks of negotiating over the latest catastrophe: Millie's injury, her own ambuscade in a Paris alleyway, and the insurance company's demanding (via Sforza) that she be replaced. Archie threatened to walk in protest after Evelyn was vetted. Now they had two leading ladies. Evelyn and Prosper rejected Wexler's first compromise, to keep Millie as Lady R and cast Nevers as Rochester's mistress Elizabeth Barry, whom Wilmot had trained as an actress and mimic, whom he'd made famous with his patronage and with whom he'd had a daughter out of wedlock that lived all of fourteen years. Madam, I am far from delighting in the grief I have given you by taking away the child; and you, who made it so absolutely necessary for me to do so, must take that excuse from me for all the ill nature of it. On the other side, pray be assured I love Betty so well that you need not apprehend any neglect from those I employ, and I hope very shortly to restore her to you a finer girl than ever.

This would have been a supporting role. Myrna, ordered to rewrite the script as quickly as possible to fit this second Elizabeth in, was as suddenly told to excise her and instead embellish the part of the Earl's formidable mother—Anne Wilmot, Countess of Rochester, a part that could be played stationary, or sitting—for Millie, demoted now from second lead billing to an additional star credit at the end of the crawl. The Countess was a fierce woman whom Rochester dreaded and did his best to avoid, leaving the old widow alone with his wife and children for months at a time while he was in town, sending sometimes conciliatory, sometimes mocking letters home to each. Dear Wife, I received your three pictures & am in a great fright lest they should be like you. By the bigness of your head, I should apprehend you far gone in the rickets; by the severity of the countenance, somewhat inclined to prayer & prophesy. Yet there is an alacrity in the plump cheek that seems to signify sack & sugar, & the sharp-sighted nose has borrowed quickness from the sweet-smelling eye. I never saw a chin smile before, a mouth frown, & a forehead mump. Truly the artist has done his part (god keep him humble), & a fine man he is if his excellencies do not puff him up like his pictures; the next impertinence I have to tell you is that I am coming down to you. I have got horses but want a coach; when that defect is supplied, you shall quickly have the trouble of—Your humble servant.

In the context of her script, Myrna put in the old woman as a hypocrite and viper, a figure of fun. Millie's role now amounted to little more than a cameo, but she was prepared to give Evelyn the fright of her life in their scenes together. Millie would be looping Evelyn's dialogue anyway, to hide her inappropriate French accent; and besides, Evelyn wasn't used to memorizing lines— Italian films didn't use sync sound, so she usually recited strings of numbers, or else nursery rhymes, as a placeholder for the real dialogue, recorded later. The great lady's vengeance would be twofold, then: she would be upstaging a girl who could only defend herself in Millie's own spooky voice. Myrna told Wexler that he had a genius for thinking up compromises that made everyone equally unhappy. There's no future in happy, he told her. These are fabulous sandwiches.

13
Selwyn Wexler

Cobblestones turn me on. Altogether I have located or located catalog entries for eleven films, or intended films, entitled *Rose Alley*; this not counting the widely available theatrical cut signed by Prosper Sforza and released to theaters for an abortive run in June 1971. A twelfth (or thirteenth?) is described in the notes (filmed) of Selwyn Wexler, these notes also entitled *Rose Alley*, constituting my latest find, en route to me from Wexler himself—along with other detritus from the winter of '69—in what I will charitably call dribs and drabs. I worry that he's tampered with them.

Classification is the first step. Classification is also the last step. Use comes in between, and is the process by which the initial organization achieves perfection in a lasting disorder. I enjoy the sorting, the putting things into categories. Correspondence here, company memos there, personal writing (doodles, cryptic reminders, shopping lists, simple equations) in pile C. Then the mother lode: old film canisters, most with yellowing receipts in them, but one or two with footage, reels from Foche's famous Bolex, absconded with by Wexler one afternoon for reasons that are likely to remain obscure. Though just as often I'll smear everything together: I have no head for organization. Things establish their own categories in time. They resonate, "not in a gross natural array," but gratifying to a more discerning sense of order. I wave my hand over my collection, in my mind, and know what belongs with which. It is a basic assumption of scholarship that certain units of information vibrate in harmony.

I have designated my finds as *RA*s 1 through 13, in the order of their discovery.

RA 1 runs five minutes and three seconds; it is Evelyn Nevers's screen test, as described earlier, and was found in a private collection (mine). The canister is labeled *Rose Alley* in black magic marker on a finger's length of now-brittle Scotch tape—though it isn't clear whether the labeler had the authority to incorporate this "scene" into the greater *Rose Alley* schema or only meant to identify the production to which the footage was attached. It was shot in January '69, when Wexler began to worry that he was turning into something distasteful. His parents had seen what they thought was their son being killed one night on the evening news. A law student, head beaten to a right angle on his neck, was strapped into a stretcher and then abandoned by panicking aid workers. Having done their mourning, they telegrammed Myrna to demand that Winnie's effects be returned. Wexler phoned to reassure them, but they insisted on quizzing him to make sure that Myrna wasn't passing off a ringer to keep the money coming. When he couldn't remember either of their birthdays, they triumphantly declared him an imposter. The letters he sent were returned. They must have moved soon after—their telephone was disconnected. And going home was out of the question. Sforza said shooting would start any day. They'd been in Paris then for most of a year.

Wexler's posture was Paleolithic: he looked like he'd been curled in a hot wind. He'd started holding grudges against people for things they'd only done in his dreams. He was afraid to go out, seeing myopic mole's eyes in the mirror and a mouth too small for articulate speech (little more, he mourned, than a beak). If between early erectus and sapiens-proper there had been a cul-de-sac species—a primate without the reptilian drive for survival, evolved too far or too purely toward cunning and cerebration—then he was its last representative: a mass of imprecise appetites, lacking the genius to define them or the apparatus to have them gratified. Evelyn's screen test had been an epiphany in this regard. He'd found himself more *involved* in the spectacle than could be healthy. He wanted so much to *do* something with it, her body—to make use of it somehow. To put it to work. Noting with diffidence that sex wasn't the entrée his nerves were calling for. There was no name for what he wanted—at least until he named it (or someone named it for him: *Wexlerisme*). He would *settle* for sex. Sex was the available substitute. Whether a sublimation or profanation of his *ism*, he couldn't say.

He was sick. He was fine. Every day some new bit of sabotage was discovered. He'd lost his leading lady to the riots and now had to contend with Evelyn, who came on to him shamelessly at every opportunity. Later, when the first day of shooting finally arrived, Wexler emerged from his barrow just long enough to frustrate Raoul into walking off the set—Winnie didn't know how to let someone else hold the camera, nor did he really know anything about the syntax of narrative film. Wexler improvised a number of setups, shooting them himself, and this resulted in several thousand feet of unexposed film going to the lab that night. After an uneventful second day's shoot, everyone but him showed up to see the first dailies at Sforza's hotel room. Sforza was tickled by the disaster and told Wexler by telegram that it was the lab's fault: try again.

RA 2 comes from the Sforza Archive, which is a pretty grand name for three filing cabinets under a tarp in a warehouse without temperature control in Trenton. I'm in the process of compiling an index for future researchers (unpaid). The footage is labeled *Rose Alley*, and, unlike the theatrical cut, credits the direction to Wexler. I suspect that it represents a work in progress left unfinished with Sforza's death in 1977. There are no titles. Screened, it looks like black leader for nearly ten minutes, but I turn up the volume, and there are voices. Finally a cut to blinding, exposed color stock—empty and untimed—engraved with florescent scratches and hairs that dance to what sounds like a Purcell song. When human beings finally come into frame, it's elbow-first, like crabs. The shots are crepuscular, as though filmed from behind a scrim, and when even a dim light is introduced, it bleaches the screen—windows, candles, and even teeth screaming white like blast furnaces. The framing is askance and obfuscatory. Dialogue is indistinct or deafening (the little speaker on my projector is wrecked now). Faces are indistinguishable from Bueno's scavenged artifacts on the walls. If those are walls. The wrong props or body parts are in sharp focus, while eyes, mouths, and hands are a mist of grain. All the data we routinely expect from a film is withheld. This *Rose Alley* is a primer as to what needs to be discarded in order for a mainstream film to be released: the secret movie that runs through every completed feature: not the discarded takes, flubbed lines, or wobbly scenery, but the outright conceptual

blunders and misunderstandings, the failed experiments, dead
time, and waste. Sequences of words are repeated; gestures are
recognized, but communicate nothing. It was almost certainly intended to be a joke. But why would Sforza expend so much time
and energy on it? And so long after the fact: hiring back Eugenia
Foche, assembling this "cut" from his fund of discarded footage?
What it most resembles is the work of some beleaguered amateurs
trying to document a haunting in their newly rented loft. No one
will ever believe them.

But on certain winter mornings, Wexler wrote me recently,
there's a white light from outside, so bright that it reflects off the
white walls of his apartment, around corners, reaching the room
where he sleeps (it's not a bedroom), harsh as artificial light, and
because of this so startling that he has to get up and walk around
that corner, to see what's going on, expecting for some reason an
accident on the street, a catastrophe outside his window, though
the light is serene and constant, like the memory of some old
humiliation. And of course it's just the usual morning light, for
some reason so bright and white that it makes a noise, and this not
a pleasant sound—that squealing you hear when you fry something porous and doughy—though a lovely invigorating sight, the
brightness, which also shows Wexler how much he needs to haul
out the vacuum, since on his white or beige carpets there are in-
numerable specks and clots that were invisible by lamplight, or
dead bugs or lint from his pockets, or in any event things that
break up the usually clean, pleasing expanse of the carpeting,
which anyway he loathes—carpets—he prefers wood.

RA 3 supposedly runs over seven hours long. The single surviving print is in the possession of Myrna Krause, who refuses to
allow it to be screened. Her *L*-shaped apartment is roughly 1,300

square feet and is accessible by fire escape via a single-hung sash window with a simple latch on the northeast corner. And did I know that Prosper even had her compose a few cues for the finished picture? She wasn't sure if they'd made it into the finished version, since she'd never seen it. Her cut has dialogue but no music. Apparently each cast member spoke his or her lines in their own language; if this version didn't go through post-production, it means that only about a third of it is in English. Given the length of the "Krause Cut," it isn't unreasonable to surmise that every page of Myrna's unwieldy script was actually filmed during the abortive three weeks of principle photography—which must surely be a record of some kind. Every page, that is, or none. Wexler tried his idea of having the cast write their own dialogue out on Myrna, armed in advance with a speech about how this was in no way a reflection on her work. Everyone would be assigned homework. "Homework?" they'd groan. But this would be turning waste into capital, using the ongoing hiatus for research. The shoot might never start, but meanwhile we can all learn a thing or two. Sure, she said—throw the script out completely. Screenplays are reactionary. He stood staring at the waistline of her jeans as she kneeled in front of their bed, working. The typewriter was set on a breakfast tray on top of their mussed sheets and blankets. Her belt, the line of the wide, studded belt on her hips, was painfully straight, remorseless. Just shy of being boyish. A perfect demarcation. Such details made Wexler feel limp and dependent. She typed gallingly slow, using only two fingers, and the contraption was antic on its raft with each letter, every carriage return threatening to capsize the machine onto their pillows. He shot a few minutes of it, covertly, though she must have heard the whirring. He kept begging her to buy a desk. When she moved, the spell was broken. When she moved, it was to go out to meet someone from the movie. She took the pages with her. Using the ribbon, Wexler was able to determine that the last word she'd typed before leaving was *alimentation*. He copied down a few more letters, hoping to reconstruct an entire sentence, but gave up after he heard a key in the lock of the next apartment over. There was no one coming—no one coming to see *him*—but he replaced the ribbon anyway and sat on the mattress. On his hands.

He kept to their room when he could, watching Myrna sleep when she deigned to sleep at home (a hand always careless under the blue cotton of her pajama bottoms: her navel incongruously oblong as a fat woman's, with tapered, winking slopes; and Wexler peculiarly affected by the sight of it, its six shiny hairs on sentry— anxious goatherds by a Caucasian chasm), reading without too much remorse the letters she received from the States or the journal entries she jotted in her damp exam books; going out when too stir-crazy to sleep, catching midnight showings of French movies with dialogue he couldn't follow, conspicuous in a throng of insomniac Parisians with hogs' faces or swans'. He gossiped to himself, about himself, in the voice of an imaginary relative—an ideal aunt or *oncle Américain*—saying, "He's going to seed," and "What's to be done with Winnie?" He'd stopped drinking, smoking, jerking off. His piss smelled in the basin as though it'd been fermenting inside him. Unable to compete with rugged, middle- of-the-road mankind, he felt that he was an anomaly, set aside for extinction. He attracted attention in the streets. They stared. He might as well have had a goiter. The locals fired wisecracks into his wake when he walked by, hard shot he collected to look up in Myrna's 1903 *Cassell's New French-English Dictionary* when he got home, compiled from the best authorities in both languages.

It was no help: as far as he could tell, what they were calling him wasn't in the book. Their name for me is newly minted and chic, he said. Sixty years ago they'd have been at a loss. Even in my regression, I am cutting edge. The primitive is modern.

*RA*s 4 and 5 are in academic collections overseas. Neither has a more than oblique relationship to our subject. 4—misfiled in special collections at Wadham College, Oxford—is a twenty-minute "stag" film dating from 1916, purporting to be a "photo-drama" documentary on the much-ballyhooed debauchery in the court of Charles II. It is never identified on-screen as *Rose Alley*, though Gilbert Beltham is listed as a consultant, and I believe he's in the background of a number of scenes, playing a courtier. Curiously, given the brevity of the picture, Dryden's assault is indeed included, as a scene of random violence in a montage of other (primarily fictional) outrages that a title card informs us go EVER UNPUNISHED, ALAS—bouffanted rakes desecrating churches, smashing expensive sundials on manor lawns, getting into brawls with the local constabulary, carousing while decent people are trying to sleep, spiriting off women and returning them without their virtue, and never seeing a comeuppance. Though the tone of the intertitles is stern and moralistic, this is clearly an exploitation film, focusing mainly on topless women and reaction shots of courtiers in flaking pancake makeup with black wine dribbling out of their mouths. 5 is at the Cinémathèque Française, again labeled *Rose Alley*, and hidden under the same catalog number as a beautiful, unscreened print of the 1971 theatrical cut, presumably because no one would ever think to look for it there. It too is silent, and the crude, handwritten title card at the beginning reads *Fantômas contre de Gaulle*. Persons unknown, probably students or volunteers once employed in the Cinémathèque itself, stole and butchered one of the few remaining original prints of a 1914 crime serial in order to make this absurdist half-hour comedy—as prank, sabotage, revolutionary action, or conscienceless vandalism. The intertitles are quotations from headlines circa the May riots, in various hands, some more legible than others, while the action itself is a now-incomprehensible mishmash of black-clad figures walking on rooftops and committing (I presume) terrible crimes, while handsome, ineffectual public servants are shown repeating the same farcically insignificant actions over and over again (slitting open a letter, reading it, passing it to a side-kick, putting their fingers to their lips in thought): befuddled and impotent forever. If only.

RA 6 isn't a film at all. It's a screenplay in manuscript, attributed to surrealist Robert Desnos (1900–1945), written sometime prior to World War II. It is a series of short, numbered paragraphs describing prospective "shots." It isn't clear to me whether it was ever intended to be filmed. Though only ten pages long, this *Rose Alley* bears more than a passing similarity to the theatrical cut of Wexler and Sforza's film, hinging as it does on Dryden's attack, likewise attributing it to a conspiracy authored by Rochester (despite the absence of evidence), and likewise inferring some kind of abstruse moral from the event, following it with Rochester's early death from complications related to debauchery and Dryden's limping on with hardly a pause to take his place in the pantheon of great English poets—though Desnos sets his script in a nineteenth-century poetry salon, doesn't name his characters, and obscures the clear movement of the plot by having the story jump from character to character as they encounter and then rendezvous with one another, only touching on his principles (THE POET and THE PATRON) as they happen to come into contact with these incidental protagonists. Finally, the daisy chain returns us to our point of departure. Also, THE POET turns into a rubber ball after his beating and bounces away over the London cobblestones. THE PATRON, on his deathbed, is discovered to have changed into a blackberry bush.

RA 7 is a catalog entry at UC Berkeley Film School. Sheryl the librarian reports that the print was stolen or destroyed during a demonstration in the mid-seventies. It may not deserve a number of its own: it could easily be a duplicate of another *Rose Alley* on this list.

I traded a print I had made of Evelyn's screen test to a connoisseur for *RA*s 8 and 9, which were missing from the Sforza Archives. It completed the connoisseur's collection of Nevers rarities. He asked me how to contact Wexler when I told him about my research, on account both of Wexler's connection to Nevers and an abiding love of his only other directorial credit, *The Gas-Pump Girls Meet the Radioactive Mummy* (1976), also produced by the jocular Sforza. I said I hadn't been able to find him.

Wexler makes a lot of promises, but it takes months for him to answer my letters. Finally a cardboard box will arrive, apparently recycled from some kind of book club, sealed with packing tape. *The Great Battles of the African Campaign Collection.* Torn ad for a biography of Rommel at a special discount gummed on one of the flats. Piece of someone's fingernail too. Inside are notebooks and loose, ruled pages. They don't look half-a-century old. He assures me, though, that they're genuine. The handwriting is his. Kept them in a safe place, he says. No light, no air. It's how he tries to live. Observed from an early age, he wrote, when I asked, initially, for an interview. Parents didn't know how best, etc. They'd never wanted children. Until they did. But ill frequently, by way of biographical detail. Ear infections. Every flu. Anxious. Cagey. So under observation. Kind of child psychology. Kind of medications. Kind of crude stuff they gave him. Warm wax medals over the eyes. That's a kind of metaphor. They used to make him keep a journal. They'd collect the notebooks every week and change his dosage depending on what they read. Or the drug. Too aggressive? Tranked him down. Short sentences, long sentences. They did close readings. All part of the diagnosis. He was operating on his brain by writing. He figured out what was going on. Wexler wasn't dumb. You learn to consider your words. Spent years on his handwriting. Perfecting it awful. But it didn't make a difference. They eased back on the X, gave him Y to clear his head. So it's hard to do even this, for you, is the point, he wrote. Have to force it out. Mainly don't answer letters. Oh, he can sign checks all right. A squiggle on the endorsement line. But bills pile up, he says—pile the verb that's stuck to noun bill nowadays. And there's a car in his driveway that he hasn't registered, hasn't even driven, except to have driven it home. Under certain conditions, we feel the measured passage of historic time to be altered, or to stop entirely. Wexler aspires to having no kind of life. It takes discipline.

Waiting with one blade of the venetian blinds raised, I watch until the mail comes. I watch through the slats, a letterbox view of the letterbox. The quality of light is identical to that which Wexler describes. Are we in the same town?

RA 8 is an hour of raw footage of what used to be called "European Market Shots": extra scenes of Evelyn Nevers and various extras lounging on settees in advanced stages of undress; filmed in a studio in Italy, with a local crew, months after the Paris shoot was closed down. Another of Eugenia's jobs was to combine Wexler's footage and this new material; which, strictly speaking, has no place in a Restoration drama, and could be more easily inserted into a picture on any of your more unregenerate Roman emperors.

9 is a collection of lighting tests made by Raoul Foche. Nevers—and Archie and Millie, and the Czechoslovakian Dryden too—pose in a number of costumes. Ball gown, housedress, lingerie, riding suit. But, then: black leather leotard and motorcycle helmet. Jeans, plaid shirt, and tasseled vest. Tinfoil armor and ray gun. T-shirt and cycling shorts. Where could these have fit in the film? Were they ever meant to be included?

All that remains of *RA* 10 is an audio track recorded by Cannon Films, who for reasons of their own picked up the Sforza Cut for American distribution and then decided to re-loop the dialogue. It's quick, shoddy work. Sounds as though it was recorded underwater. The light touch of unintentional (or unavoidable) anachronism evident in the film is here compounded by emendations in the dialogue evidently meant to give the movie more of a grindhouse flavor than the visuals alone were supplying. Long stretches sound like nothing more than two adulterers having awkward phone-sex: detailing just how wet or hard they are by turns ("so," "very"), and describing what they'd be up to if only—in this case—their bodies weren't already committed to the actions filmed years earlier in Paris.

11 is actually a forty-minute television documentary, assembled and then archived by a cooperative that used to sell stock footage to educational filmmakers for the purpose of substantiating documentaries on periods of history too remote to be cheaply recreated. Prints are still held by WNYC, a public television station in New York City. Though copyright problems have made the coop close its doors temporarily, the executive officers responded to my

inquiries promptly and with great courtesy. They invited me to tour their facilities. Gray machines enclosed by metal scaffolding work to dehumidify the vaults. They've amassed thousands of hours of footage and can provide you with everything from the dawn of creation (a bearded septuagenarian Jehovah in white muslin visiting His mostly naked playmates in the Garden—or else volcanoes and stop-motion dinosaurs with felt teeth and seams) onward (plastic windowless cities, rockets with sparkler exhausts and spiral descents, boxing kangaroos, four emaciated horsemen galloping no horses in front of rear-projection). The documentary, intended to be sold to British television, uses scenes from *Rose Alley*, as well as a number of other, better movies, as a backdrop for Archie Harkness's oleaginous narration of the events following Charles II's return to England. Harkness considered it a fitting retribution to end his life doing voice-over work for children's television and animated films. A couple of generations grew up with him as their voice of authority concerning the past. In the past, we saw, the ways people had of pretending to live in the past were ridiculous. We know better now how to do it.

Harkness had contributed to a similar piece on Cromwell and the Protectorate a few months before. Of *RA*'s principals, only Dryden is mentioned: Harkness reads some of his poem "Annus Mirabilis," describing the Great Fire, while we're shown burning stables and panicked crowds—from a western and a monster movie, respectively. Numbers onscreen tally the lives lost. The origin of the conflagration is indicated with an animated candle flame on an ancient map of London. I can't find Rose Alley, the street, even on freeze frame. I've been to London once, but that was a very long time ago.

Wexler's film diaries are *RA* 12. His weight fluctuates greatly between installments. There are shaky Paris street scenes, and passersby *do* stare. Sometimes he's following Myrna. With other people she laughs like she never does around him. How differently she moves, etc. And then his visit to Evelyn's. He should have known better than to bring the camera. It sits on a dresser, the trigger wedged in. The room is dark. You can just see Wexler hiding under her bed after he came spontaneously before she could even undress him. She walks pink to retrieve the open bottle of wine from the kitchen, and Wexler—for all I know still under that bed—speaks then in crackly VO about yet another *Rose Alley*, an uber-*Alley* that he's been considering in the interim. An aggregate *Alley*, containing all the others: its disparate parts struggling to tear away from one another while struggling, simultaneously, to integrate. An exhaustive film, depleting every possible approach to the material: at once document and fabrication, direct and oblique, projectile and shelter, kangaroo and pouch, incidental and anecdotal, tastefully vague and grotesquely precise, an escapist bromide and an incitement to riot. The dead shall live, the living die. Music shall untune the sky. On the bus, to and from the post office, Wexler watches the marquees for it. I've changed my mind and will give out his address to any interested parties.

INDEX

ACKNOWLEDGMENTS

This book contains several brief quotations, many of which may be tracked by use of the index, which was assembled by Sarah McHone-Chase.

Use of the following works is gratefully acknowledged: Graham Greene's *Lord Rochester's Monkey*, Charles Norman's *Rake Rochester*, Jeremy Treglown's edition of *Rochester's Letters*, David M. Vieth's edition of John Wilmot's *Complete Poems*, James Anderson Winn's *John Dryden and His World*, and Andrew Feenberg and Jim Freedman's *When Poetry Ruled the Streets*.

Special thanks are due the work of Professor Steven N. Zwicker of Washington University in St. Louis, and Counterpath Press.

Thanks too are due to the following individuals for the aid and comfort provided the author during the composition and publication of this book:

M. S. Atwell, David A. Davies, Judy E. Davies, K. Grossman, A D Jameson, Aude Jeanson, Steve Katz, Marshall N. Klimasewiski, Sara Malgeri, Theodore McDermott, Po Petz, Marleen Reimer, Yuriy Tarnawsky, and Hilda and Benjamin Zauderer.